MAIGRET HESITATES

MAIGRET

GEORGES SIMENON

HESITATES

Translated from the French by Lyn Moir

A HARVEST BOOK
A HELEN AND KURT WOLFF BOOK
HARCOURT BRACE & COMPANY
San Diego   New York   London

Requests for permission to make copies
of any part of the work should be mailed to:
Permissions Department,
Harcourt Brace & Company, 8th Floor,
Orlando, Florida 32887.

Maigret is a trademark of the Estate of Georges Simenon.

Library of Congress Cataloging-in-Publication Data
Simenon, Georges, 1903–1989
Maigret hesitates.
Translation of: Maigret hésite.
"A Helen and Kurt Wolff book."
"A Harvest book"
I. Title.
PQ2637.I53M26613   1986   843'.912   86-9814
ISBN 0-15-655152-7 (pbk.)

Printed in the United States of America

First Harvest edition 1986

B C D E F

MAIGRET HESITATES

1

"Hello, Janvier."

"Good morning, Chief."

"Good morning, Lucas. Good morning, Lapointe. . . ."

Maigret couldn't keep back a smile as he reached the latter. Not only because young Lapointe was wearing a slim-fitting new suit, pale gray with tiny flecks of red. Everyone was smiling that morning, in the streets, in the buses, in the shops.

The day before had been a gray and windy Sunday, with wintry squalls of rain, and suddenly, although it was only the fourth of March, they had wakened to find it was spring.

The sun was still a bit sharp, certainly, and the blue sky brittle, but there was a gaiety in the air, in the eyes of the passers-by, a sort of complicity in the *joie de vivre* and in recognizing anew the delicious smells of Paris in the morning.

Maigret had come out without a coat and had walked a good part of the way. As soon as he had come into the office he had opened the window. The Seine had changed color too; the red lines on the funnels of the tugs were brighter, the barges like new again.

He had opened the door of the inspectors' office.

"Are you coming in, boys?"

It was what they called the "little briefing," in contrast to the real briefing, which got all the divisional superintendents together with the big chief. Maigret called his closest associates together.

"Did you have a good day yesterday?" he asked Janvier.

"We took the children to my mother-in-law's, at Vaucresson."

Lapointe, uncomfortable in his new suit, which was a little too summery, kept in the background.

Maigret sat down at his desk, filled a pipe, and began to go through his mail.

"That's for you, Lucas. It's about the Lebourg case."

He held some other papers out to Lapointe.

"Take these to the Public Prosecutor's Office."

You couldn't say there was foliage yet, but there was just a touch of pale green on the trees along the quay.

There was no big case on at the moment, none of those cases that filled the hallways of the Criminal Police with reporters and photographers and which provoked peremptory telephone calls from high places. Only ordinary things. Cases to be followed up . . .

"A madman, or a madwoman," he pronounced as he picked up an envelope on which his name and the address of the Quai des Orfèvres were written in block capitals.

The envelope was white, of good quality. The stamp was canceled with the postmark of the post office in the Rue de Miromesnil. What struck the superintendent first, on pulling the letter out, was the paper, a thick, crackly vellum of an unusual shape. Someone must have cut off an engraved letterhead, and this task had been done with care, using a ruler and a very sharp knife.

The text of the letter, like the address, was in very regular block capitals.

"Perhaps not such a madman," he growled.

"Dear Divisional Superintendent,

"I do not know you personally, but what I have read of your investigations and of your attitude to criminals gives me confidence. This letter will astonish you. Do not throw it into the waste-paper basket too quickly. It is not a joke, nor is it the work of a maniac.

"You know better than I do that the truth is not always credible. A murder will be committed shortly, certainly within a few days. Perhaps by someone known to me, perhaps by me myself.

"I am not writing to you so that the murder will not take place. It is in a way inevitable. But when it happens I would like you to know.

"If you take me seriously, please put the following advertisement in the personal column of *Le Figaro* or *Le Monde*: 'K.R. I am waiting for a second letter.'

"I do not know if I shall write it. I am very worried. Certain decisions are hard to make.

"I may perhaps see you one day, in your office, but then we shall be on opposite sides of the fence.

"Yours faithfully."

*

5

He wasn't smiling any more. Frowning, he gave the sheet of paper another glance, then looked at his associates.

"No, I don't think it's a madman," he repeated. "Listen."

He read it to them, slowly, emphasizing certain words. He had had letters of this kind before, but most of the time the language was less well chosen and usually certain phrases had been underlined. They were often written in red or green ink and many of them had spelling mistakes.

The hand had not trembled here. The strokes were firm, with no flourishes or erasures.

He held the paper up to the light and read the watermark: Morvan Vellum.

He got hundreds of anonymous letters every year. With very rare exceptions, they were written on cheap paper sold at any corner store, and sometimes the words were cut out of newspapers.

"No specific threat," he murmured. "A sense of hopeless distress . . . *Le Figaro* and *Le Monde,* two daily papers read largely by the intellectual bourgeoisie . . ."

He looked at all three men again.

"Will you see to it, Lapointe? The first thing to do is to get in touch with the paper manufacturer, who must be somewhere in the Morvan."

"Right, Chief."

That was the beginning of a case which was going to give Maigret more worries than many front-page crimes.

"Put the advertisement in."

"In the *Figaro?*"

"In both papers."

A bell rang for the briefing, the real one, and Maigret, file in hand, went to the director's office. Here too the open window was letting the sounds of the city steal in. One of the superintendents was sporting a sprig of mimosa in his buttonhole, and he felt obliged to explain:

"They're selling them in the street for some charity. . . ."

Maigret did not mention the letter. His pipe was good. He watched the faces of his colleagues lazily as they set out the details of their cases in turn, and he made a mental calculation of the number of times he had been present at the same ceremony. Thousands.

But much more often he had envied the divisional superintendent who had been his chief, as he went every morning to the holy of holies. Wouldn't it be wonderful to be Chief of the Crime Squad? He hadn't dared to dream of that then, no more than Lapointe or Janvier or even Lucas did now.

It had happened all the same, and after so many years he didn't even think about it any more, except on a morning like this, when the air smelled sweet and when, instead of swearing at the roar of the buses, people smiled.

When he got back to his office half an hour later, he was surprised to find Lapointe there, standing in front of the window. His fashionable suit made him look thinner, taller, much younger. Twenty years before, a detective-inspector wouldn't have been allowed to dress like that.

"That was almost too easy, Chief."

7

"You found who makes the paper?"

"Géron and Sons, who have had the Morvan Paper Mills at Autun for three or four generations. It's not a factory—it's all done by craftsmen. The paper is hand-made, whether it's for de luxe editions, usually books of poems, it seems, or for writing paper. The Gérons have no more than ten people working there. From what I was told, there are still a few paper mills like that in the region."

"Did you get the name of their agent in Paris?"

"They don't have an agent. They work directly with art publishers and with two stationers, one on Rue du Faubourg-Saint-Honoré, the other on Avenue de l'Opéra."

"Isn't that right at the top of Rue du Faubourg-Saint-Honoré, on the left?"

"I think so, from the address. . . . The Papeterie Roman."

Maigret knew it because he had often stopped in front of the window. There were invitations there, and visiting cards, and one could read names there that one doesn't usually come across:

> *The Comte and Comtesse de Vaudry*
> *have the honor to . . .*

> *The Baronne de Grand-Lussac*
> *has the pleasure of announcing . . .*

Princes and dukes, real or not—one wondered if such people still existed. They invited each other to dinner, to shoots, to bridge parties, they announced the marriage of their daughters or the birth of a child, all on sumptuous paper.

In the other window one could admire desk blotters with armorial bearings, engagement books bound in morocco.

"You'd better go and see them."

"Roman?"

"I think it's the more likely district."

The shop on Avenue de l'Opéra had a quality trade, but it also sold fountain pens and ordinary stationery.

"I'm off, Chief."

Lucky man! Maigret watched him go like a schoolboy watching one of his friends sent on an errand by the teacher. He had only the usual drudgery to do, paperwork, always paperwork, quite devoid of interest, for a magistrate who would file it without reading it because the case was closed.

The smoke from his pipe began to turn the air blue, and a light breeze came in off the Seine, making the papers flutter. By eleven o'clock Lapointe, full of high spirits, bursting with life, came into the office.

"It's still too easy."

"What do you mean?"

"Anyone would think he'd chosen that paper on purpose. By the way, the Papeterie Roman isn't owned by Monsieur Roman any more—he died ten years ago—but by a Madame Laubier, a widow in her fifties. She would hardly let me get away. . . . She hasn't ordered any paper of that quality for five years—no one was buying it. It's not only too expensive, it doesn't take typing well.

"She still had three customers for it. One of them died last year, a count with a château in Normandy and a racing stable. His widow lives in Cannes and has never ordered any writing paper. There was also an embassy, but when the ambassador was recalled the new one ordered a different paper. . . ."

"There's still one customer?"

"There's still one customer, and that's why I say it's too easy. It's a Monsieur Emile Parendon, a lawyer on Avenue Marigny. He has been using this paper for more than fifteen years and won't have any other. Does that name mean anything to you?"

"I've never heard it. Has he ordered any recently?"

"The last time was last October."

"Headed?"

"Yes, very tastefully. Always a thousand sheets and a thousand envelopes."

Maigret picked up the telephone.

"Get me Maître Bouvier, please."

A lawyer he had known for more than twenty years, whose son also was a member of the Bar.

"Hello, Bouvier? Maigret here. Are you busy at the moment?"

"Never too busy to speak to you."

"I'd like some information."

"Confidential, of course."

"Just between the two of us, that's right. Do you know a colleague of yours called Emile Parendon?"

Bouvier seemed surprised.

"What in heaven's name can the Criminal Police have against Parendon?"

"I don't know. Probably nothing."

"That's most likely. I haven't met Parendon more than five or six times in my life. He hardly sets foot in the Law Courts and then only for civil cases. . . ."

"How old is he?"

"No age. He might just as easily be forty as fifty."

He must have turned to his secretary.

"Look up Parendon's date of birth in the Bar Yearbook. . . . Emile . . . There's only one, anyway."

Then, to Maigret:

"You must have heard of his father, who's still alive, or if he's dead it's only recently . . . Professor Parendon, the surgeon at Laënnec . . . A member of the Academy of Medicine, of the Academy of Ethical and Political Sciences, etc., etc. . . . A character. When I see you next I'll tell you about him. He came to Paris very young, with the hay still in his ears. He was short and stocky and looked like a bull . . . and he didn't just look like one. . . ."

"What about his son?"

"He's a jurist, really. He specializes in International Law, particularly in Maritime Law. They say he's unbeatable there. People come from all over the world to consult him, and he's often asked to arbitrate in delicate cases where big business interests are at stake."

"What kind of man is he?"

"Humdrum. I don't think that I'd recognize him in the street."

"Is he married?"

"Thank you, my dear. . . . There. . . . I have his age here. Forty-six. Is he married? I was going to say I didn't know, but it's coming back to me. He certainly is married —very well married, too! He married one of the daughters of Gassin de Beaulieu. . . . You remember him. . . . He was one of the most ferocious prosecutors at the time of the Liberation. Then he was appointed First President of the Supreme Court of Appeal. He must have retired to his château in the Vendée now. The family is very rich. . . ."

"Do you know anything else?"

"What else would I know? I've never had to defend them in a summary court or at the assizes. . . ."

"Do they go out a lot?"

"The Parendons? Not in my circles, anyway."

"Thanks a lot."

"You can do the same for me sometime."

Maigret reread the letter that Lapointe had laid on his desk. He reread it twice, three times, and each time he looked more somber.

"Do you know what all this means?"

"Yes, Chief. A smear. That's a strong word, but . . ."

"It's probably too mild. A noted surgeon, a First President, a specialist in Maritime Law who lives on Avenue Marigny and uses the most expensive writing paper . . ."

The kind of trouble Maigret feared most. He already had the feeling that he was walking on eggs.

"Do you think he wrote that . . . ?"

"He or someone in his household. Someone who had access to his writing paper, in any case."

12

"It's odd, isn't it?"

Maigret, who was looking out of the window, didn't answer. As a rule, people who write anonymous letters don't make a habit of using their own writing paper, particularly when it's a rather rare kind.

"Too bad. I'll have to go and see him."

He looked up the telephone number in the directory and put the call through on the outside line. A woman's voice answered.

"Maître Parendon's secretary speaking."

"Good morning, Mademoiselle. This is Superintendent Maigret of Criminal Police. Would it be possible for me to speak to Maître Parendon? I don't want to interrupt him."

"Just a moment, please. I'll find out."

It was the easiest thing in the world. Almost immediately a man's voice said:

"This is Parendon."

There was a questioning note in his voice.

"I wanted to ask you, Maître . . ."

"Who is that speaking? My secretary didn't quite catch your name."

"Superintendent Maigret."

"I can understand her surprise now. She must have heard properly, but she didn't imagine it was really you who . . . I'm delighted to be speaking to you, Monsieur Maigret. . . . I've often thought of you. . . . I've even been on the point of writing to you to ask your opinion on certain matters. . . . I haven't dared, knowing you to be such a busy man. . . ."

Parendon had a timid voice, yet it was Maigret who was the more embarrassed of the two. He felt ridiculous now, with his meaningless letter.

"Now I'm the one who is disturbing you. And for a mere trifle, in the bargain. I would prefer to speak to you in person, as I have a document I would like to show you."

"When would you like to come?"

"Have you got a free moment sometime this afternoon?"

"Would three thirty be convenient? I must confess that I usually take a short siesta and I feel terrible if I don't have it."

"Three thirty will be fine. I'll come to your house. Thank you for being so helpful."

When Maigret put down the receiver he looked at Lapointe as if he were waking up from a dream.

"Didn't he seem surprised?"

"Not in the least. He didn't ask any questions. He says he's quite looking forward to meeting me. There's one thing that intrigues me. He says he has been on the point of writing to me for an opinion more than once. Now, he doesn't plead in the criminal courts, only in the civil courts. His specialty is Maritime Law, about which I don't know a thing. What does he want my opinion on?"

Maigret told a small lie that day. He telephoned his wife and told her that he was held up at work. He wanted to celebrate the spring sunshine by having lunch at the Brasserie Dauphine, where he even treated himself to a *pastis* at the bar.

If there was muckraking to be done, as Lapointe had hinted, at least it was beginning pleasantly.

Maigret had taken the bus to the Rond-Point, and in the hundred yards he walked along Avenue Marigny he saw at least three faces he thought he recognized. He had forgotten that he was walking alongside the gardens of the Elysée Palace and that the area was heavily guarded day and night. The guardian angels recognized him too and gave him a discreet and respectful salute.

The building where Parendon had his apartment was vast and solid, built to defy the passage of time. The gateway was flanked by bronze candelabra. From the entrance one could see that the concierge did not have the usual little room, but a veritable drawing room, with a table covered with green velvet, as if it were in a Ministry.

The superintendent found a familiar face here, too, a man called Lamule or Lamure who had worked on Rue des Saussaies for many years. He was wearing a gray uniform with silver buttons, and he seemed surprised to see Maigret looming up in front of him.

"Who have you come to see, Chief?"

"Maître Parendon."

"Take the elevator or the staircase on the left. It's on the first floor."

Behind the house there was a courtyard with cars, garages, and low buildings which must have been stables once. Maigret emptied his pipe mechanically, tapping it on his heel before he started to climb the marble staircase.

When he rang at the only door, a butler in a white jacket opened it as if he had been waiting for him.

"I have an appointment with Maître Parendon."

"This way, Superintendent."

He took Maigret's hat with an air of authority and showed him into a library the like of which the superintendent had never seen before. The room was long, with a very high ceiling, and books lined the walls from floor to ceiling except where there was a marble fireplace with a bust of an oldish man on the mantelpiece. All the books were bound in leather, most of them red leather. The only pieces of furniture were a long table, two chairs, and an armchair.

He would have liked to examine the titles of the books, but a young secretary wearing glasses was already approaching him.

"Will you come this way, Superintendent?"

The sun was pouring in through windows more than nine feet high and playing on the carpets, on the furniture, on the pictures. For, from the hall on, the place was filled with antique pier tables and other period furniture, busts and paintings of gentlemen in the costumes of every age.

The girl opened a light oak door, and a man who had been sitting at his desk got up and stepped forward to greet Maigret. He too wore glasses, with very thick lenses.

"Thank you, Mademoiselle Vague."

He had to walk a long way, since the room was as big as a state reception room. Here too the walls were lined with books, there were portraits, and the sun broke up the whole into diamond patterns.

"You have no idea how happy I am to see you, Monsieur Maigret. . . ."

He held out his hand, a little white hand which felt boneless to the touch. In contrast to the décor, the man seemed even smaller than what must be his real size— small and frail and curiously light. And yet he wasn't thin. His outlines were quite rounded, but the whole effect was of weightlessness, of insubstantiality.

"Come this way, please. Let's see . . . Where would you prefer to sit?"

He pointed to a tawny leather armchair, near the desk.

"I think you would be most comfortable here. I am a little deaf. . . ."

Maigret's friend Bouvier had been right in saying that the man was of no age. He still had an almost childish expression in his face and his blue eyes, and he looked at the superintendent with a kind of wonder.

"You can't imagine the number of times I've thought of you. When you are on a case I devour several newspapers a day so that I don't miss a detail—I might almost say that I wait to see what your reactions are. . . ."

Maigret felt awkward. He had grown accustomed to the curiosity of the public, but the enthusiasm of a man like Parendon put him in an embarrassing position.

"Well, my reactions are just the same as those the average man might have in my place."

"The average man, maybe. But there is no such thing as the 'average man.' . . . That's a myth. What isn't a myth is the Penal Code, the judges, the juries. . . . And the juries who were 'average men' the day before become different people the minute they enter the courtroom."

He was wearing a dark gray suit, and the desk he was leaning on was much too big for him. But he didn't look ridiculous. Perhaps that wasn't naïveté, either, shining in the eyes behind the thick lenses of his glasses.

As a schoolboy he had perhaps had to put up with being called "half-pint," but he had resigned himself to the inevitable and he gave the impression of a benevolent gnome who had to keep his high spirits in check.

"May I ask you a rather personal question? How old were you when you began to understand men? I mean, to understand the men we call criminals?"

Maigret blushed and stammered:

"I don't know. I'm not sure that I do understand them. . . ."

"Oh yes, you do! And they know it very well. That's one of the reasons why they are almost relieved to confess."

"It's the same with my colleagues."

"I could prove the contrary by mentioning several cases, but that would only bore you. You studied medicine, didn't you?"

"Only for two years."

"If what I've read is true, your father died, and since you were unable to continue your studies you joined the police."

Maigret's position was growing more and more delicate, almost ridiculous. He had come to ask questions and he was the one being interviewed.

"I don't see a change of vocation in that, but a different way of expressing the same character. . . . Excuse me. . . . I have literally thrown myself at you since you came in. I was awaiting your arrival impatiently. I would have opened the door myself when you rang, but my wife wouldn't have liked that—she insists on a certain decorum. . . ."

His voice had lowered several tones on speaking these last words and, pointing to an immense painting depicting, almost full-length, a judge dressed in ermine, he whispered:

"My father-in-law."

"First President Gassin de Beaulieu?"

"Do you know him?"

During the last few minutes Parendon had looked so like a little boy that Maigret felt he had to admit:

"I did my homework before I came."

"Did anyone say anything against him?"

"It seems that he's a great judge."

"There you are! . . . A great judge! . . . Do you know the works of Henri Ey?"

"I've read his textbook on psychiatry."

"Sengès? Levy-Valensi? Maxwell?"

He pointed to a section of the bookshelves where the books bore these names. But they were all psychiatrists who had never taken any interest in Maritime Law. Maigret recognized other names as he glanced at them. He had seen some of them quoted in the journals of the International Society of Criminology, and he had in fact read the works of others: Lagache, Ruyssen, Genil-Perrin.

"Aren't you smoking?" his host suddenly asked him, astonished. "I thought you always had a pipe in your mouth."

"I'd rather not, thank you."

"What may I offer you? The cognac isn't particularly good, but I have a forty-year-old armagnac. . . ."

He trotted over to a wall where a section of paneling between the rows of books hid a bar with some twenty bottles and glasses of all sizes.

"Just a little, please."

"My wife only lets me have a drop on special occasions. She says I have a weak liver. According to her I'm weak all over and I haven't a single healthy organ in me."

That amused him. He spoke without bitterness.

"Your health! If I have been asking these personal questions, it is because I am passionately interested in Article 64 of the Penal Code, which you must know better than I do."

Indeed, Maigret knew it by heart. He had gone over it again and again, many times, in his mind:

"If the person charged with the commission of a felony or misdemeanor was then insane or acted by absolute necessity, no offense has been committed."

"What do you think of it?" asked the gnome, leaning toward him.

"I am glad I'm not a judge. That way, I don't have to pass judgment."

"That's the kind of thing I like to hear you say. This is the kind of thing I want to know—sitting in your office in front of a guilty man, or a man who is presumed guilty, are you capable of determining to what extent he is responsible?"

"Rarely. . . . The psychiatrists, afterwards . . ."

"This library is full of psychiatrists. The older generation, for the most part, answered 'responsible,' and went on their way with a clear conscience. But read Henri Ey again, for example. . . ."

"I know."

"Do you speak English?"

"Very badly."

"Do you know what they mean by a hobby?"

"Yes. A pastime, something one does without payment, a craze, a mania . . ."

"Well, my dear Monsieur Maigret, my hobby, my mania, as some people say, is Article 64. I'm not the only one. And that celebrated article isn't found only in the French Penal Code—in more or less identical terms it is found in the United States, in England, in Germany, in Italy. . . ."

He grew animated. His face, which had been rather pale, grew pink and he gesticulated with surprising energy.

"There are thousands of us all over the world, no, tens of thousands, who have made it our goal to change this shameful Article 64, which is a relic of the past. It's not a secret society. There are official organizations in most countries, with their magazines, journals . . . Did you know the answer they give us?"

And, as if to make the "they" more personal, he glanced at the portrait of his father-in-law.

"They tell us:

" 'The Penal Code is an integrated whole. If you tamper with one stone, the whole edifice runs the risk of collapsing.'

"They also object:

" 'If one followed your wishes, the doctor and not the judge would have the task of judging.'

"I could talk to you about it for hours. I have written many articles on the subject and I will get my secretary to send you some of them, which may seem presumptuous on my part. You know criminals, if I may say so, at first hand. As far as a judge is concerned, they are creatures who fit almost automatically into one compartment or the other. You see, don't you?"

"Yes."

"Your good health."

He drew his breath, seeming to be surprised, himself, at having got so involved.

"There aren't many people I can talk to so openly. I hope I haven't shocked you?"

"Not at all."

"In fact, I haven't even asked you why you wanted to see me. I have been so thrilled at this chance that it never even occurred to me. . . ."

And, with a touch of irony:

"I hope it's nothing to do with Maritime Law."

Maigret had taken the letter out of his pocket.

"I received this letter in this morning's mail. It has no signature. I am not at all certain that it came from this house. I would just like you to look at it."

Oddly enough, the lawyer began by feeling the paper, as if his sense of touch was the most strongly developed of his senses.

"It could be mine. . . . It's not easily come by. The last time, my engraver had to order it from the manufacturer."

"That's exactly what brought me here."

Parendon had put on a different pair of glasses, crossed his short legs, and was moving his lips as he read, uttering a few phrases in a low voice.

" 'A murder will be committed shortly. . . . Perhaps by someone known to me, perhaps by me myself.' "

He reread the paragraph carefully.

"It looks as if each word had been carefully chosen, don't you think?"

"That is the impression I got from the letter."

" 'It is, in a way, inevitable.' "

"I don't like that sentence so well. There's something gratuitous about it."

Then, holding the paper out to Maigret and changing his glasses again:

"Strange . . ."

He wasn't the man for long words, for emphasis. His commentary was restricted to that one word.

"One detail struck me," Maigret explained. "The person who wrote this letter does not address me as Superintendent, as most people do, but by my official title, Divisional Superintendent."

"I thought of that too. Have you placed the advertisement?"

"It will appear in *Le Monde* this evening and in tomorrow morning's *Figaro*."

The oddest thing was that Parendon was not surprised or, if he was, he didn't show it. He was looking out of the window at the gnarled trunk of a chestnut tree when his attention was caught by a slight noise. He was not surprised by that either. Turning his head, he murmured:

"Come in, my dear."

And, getting up:

"Let me introduce Superintendent Maigret in person."

The woman, who was about forty, elegant, very vivacious, with extremely restless eyes, took only a few seconds to examine the superintendent from head to toe. She would doubtless have noticed if he had had a tiny speck of mud on his left shoe.

"How do you do, Superintendent? I hope you haven't come to arrest my husband. With his poor health you would have to put him in the prison infirmary."

Her tone was not biting. She did not speak with any malice but she did say it, though with the gayest of smiles.

"I expect it's about one of our domestics."

"I have had no complaint about any of them. That would be a matter for the local police."

She was dying to know why he was there. Her husband knew that as well as Maigret did, but neither of them gave the slightest hint, as if they were playing a game.

"What do you think of our armagnac?"

She had removed the glasses.

"I hope you only had a drop, darling."

She was wearing a light-colored suit, a spring style although the season had only just begun.

"Oh well, gentlemen, I'll leave you to your own affairs. . . . I was going to tell you that I won't be back before eight, darling. You can always join me at Hortense's, after seven, if you like. . . ."

She did not leave immediately, but managed, while the two men remained standing silent, to make a tour of the room, changing the position of an ashtray on a pedestal table, putting a book into line with the rest.

"Good-by, Monsieur Maigret. I am so happy to have met you. You are an extremely interesting man. . . ."

The door closed behind her. Parendon sat down again. He waited a moment longer, as if he expected the door to open again. Finally he laughed, a childlike laugh.

"Did you get that?"

Maigret didn't know what to say.

" 'You are an extremely interesting man.' She is furious that you didn't say anything to her. Not only does she not know why you are here, you didn't comment on her dress or, more important, on how young she is. Nothing would have given her greater pleasure than for you to have taken her for my daughter."

"Do you have a daughter?"

Yes, she's eighteen. She has passed her *baccalauréat* and is taking some classes in archaeology—I don't know how long that will last. Last year she wanted to be a lab assistant. I don't see a lot of her except at mealtimes, when she deigns to eat with us. . . . I have a son, too, Jacques.

He's fifteen and in the third grade at the Lycée Racine.
. . . They are all the family we have."

He spoke lightly, as if the words had no importance or
as if he were poking fun at himself.

"In fact, I'm wasting your time and we ought to get
back to your letter. Wait a moment. . . . Here's a sheet of
my writing paper. Your experts will tell you if it's really
the same paper, but I am already certain that it is."

He rang a bell and waited, his head turned toward the
door.

"Mademoiselle Vague, would you be so good as to bring
me one of the envelopes we use for the tradesmen?"

He explained:

"We pay the tradespeople by check at the end of the
month. It would be pretentious to use our engraved envelopes to pay their bills. So we have ordinary white envelopes."

The girl brought one.

"You can compare them too. If the envelopes and the
paper are both the same, you can be almost certain that
the letter came from here."

That did not appear to upset him unduly.

"Can you think of any reason which might have
prompted someone to write this letter?"

He looked at Maigret, first rather bewildered, then with
a more disillusioned look.

"Reasons? I wasn't expecting that word, Monsieur
Maigret. I realize you must ask the question. But why reasons? Undoubtedly everyone has some, consciously or
not. . . ."

26

"Do many people live in this apartment?"

"Living in, not very many. My wife and I, of course. . . ."

"Do you sleep in separate bedrooms?"

He gave Maigret a swift look, as if he had scored a point.

"How did you guess?"

"I don't know. . . . I asked the question without thinking."

"It's quite true, we do sleep in separate rooms. My wife likes to go to bed late and stay in bed in the mornings, and I am an early bird. . . . In any case, you are free to go through all the rooms whenever you like. I may as well say at once that I did not choose the apartment, nor did I have anything to do with furnishing it.

"When my father-in-law"—a glance at the First President—"retired and went to live in the Vendée, there was a sort of family council. There are four daughters, all married. They more or less divided up their inheritance ahead of time, and my wife got this apartment with all its contents, including the portraits and the busts."

He neither laughed nor smiled. It was more subtle than that.

"One of the sisters will inherit the country place in the Vendée, in the Forest of Vouvant, and the other two will share the stocks and bonds. The Gassin de Beaulieus are a very wealthy old family, so there's enough for everyone.

"So I am not quite in my own home, but rather in my father-in-law's, and only the books and furniture in my bedroom and this study are my own things."

27

"Your father is still alive, isn't he?"

"He lives almost opposite, on the Rue de Miromesnil, in an apartment he furnished for his retirement. He has been a widower for thirty years. He was a surgeon. . . ."

"A famous surgeon."

"Yes. You know that too. Then you must know that his passion was not Article 64, but women. . . . We own an apartment just as big as this one, but more modern, on Rue d'Aguesseau. My brother and his wife live there. He's a neurologist.

"Now the family . . . I have already told you about my daughter Paule and her brother Jacques. If you want to get on well with her, you had better know that my daughter calls herself Bambi and insists on calling her brother Gus. I suppose that will pass. And even if it doesn't, it's not very important. . . .

"As for the domestics, as my wife would say, you have already seen Ferdinand, the butler. His surname is Fauchois. He comes from Berry, like my family. He's a bachelor. His room is on the other side of the courtyard, over the garages. Lise, the maid, sleeps in the apartment, and there is a Madame Marchand who comes in daily to do the cleaning. . . . I was forgetting the cook, Madame Vauquin—her husband is a pastry cook and she has to go home at night.

"Aren't you taking any notes?"

Maigret just smiled, then he got up and went over to a large ashtray where he emptied his pipe.

"Now, my side of the household, if I may call it that . . . You have met Mademoiselle Vague. . . . That's her real name and she doesn't find it at all ridiculous. I have always called my secretaries by their surnames. She never speaks of her private life and I would have to consult my records to find her address.

"All I know about her is that she goes home by métro and that she will do evening work without complaining. She must be about twenty-four or twenty-five and she is rarely in a bad temper.

"To help me with my briefs I have an ambitious clerk, René Tortu. His office is at the end of the hall.

"Finally there is what we call the scribe, a boy of about twenty who has just come from Switzerland. I think he has ambitions to be a playwright. He does everything. A sort of office boy.

"When I am given a case it's almost always a big one, a matter of millions, if not hundreds of millions, and then I have to work day and night for a week or more. After that we fall back on routine and I have time to . . ."

He blushed and smiled.

". . . to devote to our Article 64, Monsieur Maigret. One day you must tell me what you think of it. In the meantime, I shall let everyone know that you are to have the freedom of the apartment, and to answer all your questions truthfully."

Maigret looked at him, a bit worried. He was not sure whether he was looking at a very astute actor or, on the contrary, a poor, sickly man whose only consolation was a subtle sense of humor.

"I shall probably come in tomorrow, sometime in the morning, but I shan't disturb you."

"In that case I shall probably disturb you."

They shook hands, and the hand that the superintendent held in his own was almost that of a child.

"Thank you for receiving me so kindly, Monsieur Parendon."

"Thank you for your visit, Monsieur Maigret."

The lawyer trotted behind him as far as the elevator.

2

Once outside, he found the sun again, and the scent of the first fine days of the year. There was already a faint smell of dust. The guardian angels of the Elysée Palace walked along nonchalantly and gave him discreet signs of recognition.

At the corner of the Rond-Point, an old woman was selling lilacs which smelled like suburban gardens, and Maigret resisted the impulse to buy some. What would he have looked like arriving at the Quai des Orfèvres carrying a huge bunch of flowers?

He felt lightheaded—an odd sort of lightheadedness. He had just left a hitherto unknown world where he had found himself more like a fish out of water than he would ever have believed. As he walked along the sidewalks, among the jostling crowds, he could visualize the solemn apartment presided over by the shade of the great judge. He must have given formal receptions there.

From the start Parendon, as if to put him at his ease, had given him a sort of wink that said:

"Don't get it wrong. All this is only décor. Even the Maritime Law is only a game, only make-believe. . . ."

And he had brought out a toy, his Article 64, which interested him more than anything else in the world.

Or was Parendon a sly one? In any case, Maigret felt attracted to the skipping gnome who devoured him with his eyes as if he had never before seen a superintendent of the Criminal Police.

He took advantage of the good weather to walk down the Champs-Elysées as far as the Place de la Concorde, where he finally took a bus. He couldn't get one with a platform, so he had to put out his pipe and sit inside.

When he got back to his office it was time to sign his mail, and he took twenty minutes to get through the letters. His wife was surprised to see him come in at six o'clock, looking gay.

"What's for dinner?"

"I thought I'd cook . . ."

"Don't cook anything. We're going to eat out."

It didn't matter where, just as long as they could dine outside. It was no ordinary day, and he wanted it to stay special right to the end.

The days were growing longer. They found a restaurant in the Latin Quarter with a glassed-in terrace pleasantly warmed by a charcoal heater. The specialty of the house was sea food, and Maigret sampled almost every kind, even some sea urchins flown in that very day from the Midi.

She looked at him, smiling.

"You've had a good day, haven't you?"

"I saw a very odd man. . . . A very odd house, too, and some very odd people."

"A crime?"

"I don't know. . . . It hasn't been committed yet, but it could happen at any time. And when it does, I'll find myself in a very awkward situation."

He rarely talked to her about cases under way, and she usually learned more about them from the newspapers and the radio than from her husband. This time, he gave in to the urge to show her the letter.

"Read that."

They had reached the dessert. They had drunk a bottle of Pouilly Fumé with their grilled red mullet, and its aroma still surrounded them. Madame Maigret gave her husband a rather surprised look as she handed back the letter.

"Was it written by a child?" she asked.

"There is in fact a child in the house. I haven't seen him yet. But there are such things as childlike men. And childlike women too, when they get to a certain age."

"Is that what you think?"

"Somebody wanted me to go into that house. If he hadn't, he wouldn't have used writing paper which is sold these days only in two stationers' in Paris."

"If he's planning to commit a crime . . ."

"He doesn't say that he is going to commit a crime. He is telling me there is going to be one, and he doesn't seem to be too sure who is going to commit it."

33

For once she didn't take him seriously.

"It's just a joke, you'll see."

He paid the bill. It was so warm that they walked home, making a detour to walk through the Ile Saint-Louis.

He found lilacs on Rue Saint-Antoine, so there were some in the apartment that night, after all.

The next morning the sun was just as bright, the air just as clear, but already Maigret took less notice of it. He found Lucas, Janvier, and Lapointe ready for the little briefing, and he looked immediately for the letter in the pile of mail.

He was not sure that it would be there, for the advertisement in the *Monde* had not appeared until the middle of the previous evening, and the *Figaro* had only just come out.

"There it is!" he cried, brandishing it in the air.

The same envelope, the same carefully written block letters, the same writing paper with the letterhead cut off.

The writer didn't call him Divisional Superintendent any more, and the tone had changed.

"You made a mistake, Monsieur Maigret, in coming before receiving my second letter. Now they all have a bee in their bonnet and that means things will be speeded up. From now on, the crime may be committed at any moment, and that will be partly your fault.

"I thought you were more patient, more reflective. Do you really think that you are capable of discovering the secrets of a whole household in one afternoon?

"You are more credulous, and perhaps more vain, than I

had thought. I cannot help you any more. My only advice to you is to continue your investigation without believing what anyone tells you.

"With regards. In spite of everything I retain my admiration for you."

The three men standing facing him realized that he was embarrassed, and he handed them the sheet of paper with some reluctance. They were even more embarrassed than he was at the offhand way the anonymous correspondent was treating their chief.

"Don't you think it's a kid having fun?"

"That's what my wife said last night."

"What do you think?"

"No. . . ."

No, he didn't think that it was a joke in poor taste. Besides, there was nothing dramatic in the air on the Avenue Marigny. In that apartment everything was clear and well ordered. The butler had received him with calm dignity. The secretary with the funny name was lively and pleasant. As for Maître Parendon, he had shown himself to be a most charming host in spite of his strange appearance.

The idea that it might be a joke had not occurred to Parendon either. He had made no protest against this intrusion into his private life. He had talked a lot about many subjects, particularly about Article 64, but, after all, hadn't there been an undercurrent of unhappiness all the time?

Maigret did not mention it at the big briefing. He realized that his colleagues would shrug their shoulders if they knew he was involving himself in such an unlikely affair.

"Anything new with you, Maigret?"

"Janvier is just on the point of arresting the man who killed the postmistress. We are almost sure, but we'd better wait a bit and see if he had an accomplice. . . . He's living with a young girl, and she's pregnant. . . ."

Ordinary things. Commonplace things. Everyday things. One hour later he left the everyday world as he went into the building on Avenue Marigny. The uniformed concierge waved to him through the glass door of the lodge.

Ferdinand, the butler, took his hat and asked:

"Do you wish me to announce your arrival to Monsieur?"

"No. Take me to the secretary's office."

Mademoiselle Vague! That was it! He had remembered her name. She worked in a small room with green-painted filing cabinets around the walls, and she was typing on the latest-model electric typewriter.

"Did you want to see me?" she asked, not at all upset.

She got up, looked around her, and pointed to a chair near the window which looked onto the courtyard.

"I'm sorry I haven't got an armchair for you. If you'd rather, we could go to the library or the drawing room. . . ."

"I'd prefer to stay here."

He could hear a vacuum cleaner running somewhere in the apartment. Another typewriter was clacking away in one of the offices. A man's voice, not Parendon's, was speaking on the telephone:

"Yes, yes. . . . I understand you perfectly, my dear boy, but the law is the law, even if it sometimes runs counter to common sense. . . . I have spoken to him about it, of course. . . . No, he can't see you today or tomorrow, and that wouldn't help anyway. . . ."

"Monsieur Tortu?" Maigret asked.

She nodded. The clerk was speaking in the next room. Mademoiselle Vague went over and shut the door, cutting off the sound just as if she had turned off the radio. The window was open a little and a chauffeur in blue denims was hosing down a Rolls-Royce.

"Does that belong to Monsieur Parendon?"

"No, to the tenants on the second floor. They're Peruvians."

"Does Monsieur Parendon have a chauffeur?"

"He has to, because his eyesight is too poor to let him drive."

"What kind of car does he have?"

"A Cadillac. Madame uses it more often than he does, although she has a little English car of her own. Does the noise disturb you? Are you sure you wouldn't like me to shut the window?"

No. The jet of water was part of the atmosphere, of spring, of a house like the one he found himself in.

"Do you know why I am here?"

"I only know that we are all at your service and that we are to answer all your questions even if we think they are indiscreet."

He took the first letter out of his pocket again. He would have a photocopy made of it when he got back to the Quai, otherwise it would end up in shreds.

While she was reading it, he examined her face, which

37

her round tortoise-shell spectacles managed not to make ugly. She was not beautiful in the usual sense, but she had a pleasant face. Her mouth in particular held the eye, full, smiling, its corners turned up.

"Yes?" she said, handing back the paper.

"What do you think of it?"

"What does Monsieur Parendon think?"

"The same as you do."

"What do you mean?"

"That he was no more surprised than you are."

She forced herself to smile, but he could tell that the shot had gone home.

"Should I have reacted in any special way?"

"When someone announces that a murder is going to be committed in a house . . ."

"That could happen in any house, couldn't it? Up to the moment when a man commits a crime, I suppose that he acts like any other man, that he is like any other man, otherwise . . ."

"Otherwise we would arrest future criminals in advance. That's true enough."

The strange thing was that she had thought of that, for few people in the course of Maigret's long career had given him that simple piece of reasoning.

"I put the advertisement in. This morning I had a second letter."

He held it out to her, and she read it with the same attention, but this time with a certain anxiety too.

"I'm beginning to understand," she murmured.

"What?"

"Why you are worried and why you are taking on the investigation yourself."

"May I smoke?"

"Please do. I am allowed to smoke in here, which isn't the case in most offices."

She lit a cigarette with simple, unaffected gestures, unlike so many women. She smoked in order to relax. She leaned back a little in her secretary's chair. The office did not look at all like a business office. Although the typewriter table was metal, an extremely beautiful Louis XIII table stood beside it.

"Is the Parendon boy a practical joker?"

"Gus? He's quite the opposite. He is intelligent, but reserved. He is always at the top of his class at the lycée, though he never does any work."

"What is he most interested in?"

"Music and electronics. He has built a complete hi-fi system in his bedroom, and he subscribes to I don't know how many scientific magazines. . . . Look, here's one that came in this morning's mail. I'm the one who puts them in his room."

Electronics of Tomorrow.

"Does he go out a lot?"

"I'm not here in the evenings. I don't think so."

"Has he any friends?"

"Sometimes a friend comes to listen to records or to do experiments with him."

"How does he get on with his father?"

She seemed surprised by the question. She thought for a moment, and smiled to excuse herself.

"I don't know what to say. I have been working for Monsieur Parendon for five years. It's only my second job in Paris."

"Where was the first?"

"In a business on Rue Réaumur. I wasn't happy, because the work didn't interest me."

"Who got you this post?"

"René. I mean Monsieur Tortu. He told me about this job."

"Did you know him well?"

"We used to have our evening meal at the same restaurant on the Rue Caulaincourt."

"Do you live in Montmartre?"

"On the Place Constantin-Pecqueur."

"Was Tortu your . . . *petit-ami?*"

"First of all, he's not so little—almost six foot three. Anyway, except for one time, there hasn't been anything between us."

"Except for one time?"

"I've been told to be absolutely frank, haven't I? . . . One evening, not long before I came here, we went to the movies together on the Place Clichy, after we left 'Chez Maurice'—'Chez Maurice,' that's the restaurant on Rue Caulaincourt. . . ."

"Do you still eat there?"

"Almost every evening. I'm part of the furniture."

"And he?"

"Not so often now that he's engaged."

"So, after the movies . . ."

"He asked me if he could come up and have a drink at

my apartment. We'd already had a few drinks, and I was a little bit drunk. I said no, because I hate the idea of a man coming into my room. . . . It's something physical. . . . I said I'd go with him to his apartment on the Rue des Saules. . . ."

"Why didn't it happen again?"

"Because it didn't work out, we both realized that. . . . Just one of those things, in fact . . . We're still good friends."

"Is he going to get married soon?"

"I don't think he's in any hurry. . . ."

"Is his fiancée a secretary too?"

"She's Dr. Parendon's, the boss's brother's, assistant."

Maigret smoked his pipe in short puffs, trying to soak up everything about this world which he had not known anything about the previous day, and which had just welled up in his life.

"Since we're talking about such things, I'm going to ask you another indiscreet question. Do you go to bed with Monsieur Parendon?"

It was her way of doing things. She listened attentively to the question, her face serious. She took her time and then, at the moment of answering, she began to smile, a smile both mischievous and spontaneous, while her eyes twinkled behind her glasses.

"In a sense, yes. We make love, but it's always on the run, so to speak, so the word 'bed' isn't appropriate, since we've never been to bed together."

"Does Tortu know?"

"We've never spoken about it, but he must guess."

"Why?"

"When you know the apartment better, you'll understand. Let's see, how many people are around here during the day? . . . Monsieur and Madame Parendon and the two children, that's four. Three in the office, seven. Ferdinand, the cook, the maid, and the cleaning-woman, brings us to eleven. Not to mention Madame's masseur, who comes four mornings a week, or her sisters, or her friends. . . . Even though there are a lot of rooms, one meets everyone else. Especially in here."

"Why in here especially?"

"Because it's in here everyone comes to get paper, stamps, paper clips. . . . If Gus needs a piece of string, it's these drawers he comes to look in. . . . Bambi always needs stamps or scotch tape. As for Madame . . ."

He watched her, curious to see how she would continue.

"She's everywhere. Oh, yes, she goes out a lot, but one never knows if she's out or in. You will have noticed that all the halls and most of the rooms are carpeted. You can't hear anyone coming. The door opens and in pops someone you weren't expecting. For example, she sometimes pushes open my door and mutters 'Oh, excuse me,' as if she'd made a mistake. . . ."

"Is she inquisitive?"

"Or scatterbrained. Unless she has a thing about it."

"Has she never surprised you with her husband?"

"I'm not sure. Once, not long before Christmas, when we thought she was at the hairdresser's, she came in at a rather delicate moment. We had time to look normal, at least I think we did, but I'm not sure. She seemed very natural and began to talk to her husband about the present she had just bought for Gus."

"Hasn't she changed in her attitude to you?"

"No. She is nice to everyone, a kind of niceness that is peculiarly her own, a little as if she were floating around above us to protect us. . . . I've secretly nicknamed her the angel. . . ."

"Don't you like her?"

"I wouldn't have her for a friend, if that's what you mean."

A bell rang, and the girl got up suddenly.

"Will you excuse me? The boss is calling me."

She was at the door already, having picked up a pencil and a shorthand notebook on the way.

Maigret remained alone, watching the chauffeur in the courtyard not yet reached by the sun. He was polishing the Rolls with a chamois and whistling a catchy tune.

Mademoiselle Vague did not come back, and Maigret remained seated by the window—he who had such a horror of waiting. He could have gone along to the end of the hall to the office occupied by Tortu and Julien Baud, but it was as if he were in a pleasant stupor, his eyes half closed, looking first at one thing, then at another.

The table that served as a desk had heavy oak legs, tastefully carved, and it must have stood previously in another room. Its surface was polished by long use. There was a beige blotter with four leather corners. The pen-tray was

43

very ordinary, made of a kind of plastic. It held fountain pens, pencils, a rubber, and a scraping knife. There was a dictionary near the typing table.

Suddenly he frowned. He stood up rather regretfully and went over to look more closely at the table. He had not been mistaken. There was a thin cut, still fresh, such as the erasing-knife would have made cutting a sheet of paper.

Near the pen-tray there was a flat metal ruler.

"You've noticed that too?"

He jumped. It was Mademoiselle Vague who had come in, still holding her notebook.

"What do you mean?"

"The scratch. Isn't it awful to spoil such a lovely table?"

"Have you any idea who did it?"

"Anyone with access to this room, that is to say, anyone at all. I told you everybody treated this place as his own."

So he wouldn't have to search. He had promised himself the previous day that he would examine all the tables in the house, for he had noticed that the paper has been cut cleanly, as if with a guillotine.

"Did you tell him what we were talking about?"

She answered, not in the least embarrassed:

"Yes."

"Even about your relationship with him?"

"Of course."

"Is that why he called you?"

"No. He really had something to ask me about the case he's working on just now."

"I'll come back in a moment. I suppose you don't need to show me in any more?"

She smiled.

"He told you to make yourself at home, didn't he?"

So he knocked at the tall oak door, opened it, and found the little man sitting at his desk, which was covered this morning with official-looking documents.

"Come in, Monsieur Maigret. I'm sorry I interrupted you. I didn't know you were with my secretary. You're getting to know a bit more about our household.

"Would it be indiscreet to ask you if I could look at the second letter?"

Maigret gave it to him willingly, and he had the impression that Parendon's face, which was already colorless, grew waxy. The blue eyes no longer sparkled behind the thick glasses, but stared at Maigret with an anguished, questioning look.

" 'From now on, the crime may be committed at any moment.' Do you believe that?"

Maigret, who was staring at him equally hard, said only:

"Do you?"

"I don't know. I don't know any longer. Yesterday I took the affair rather lightly. Although I did not believe it was a spiteful joke, I was tempted to think it was a minor revenge, treacherous and naïve at the same time. . . ."

"Against whom?"

"Against me, against my wife, against anyone in the house. . . . A clever way of getting the police here and having us harassed by questions."

"Have you mentioned it to your wife?"

"I had to, since she met you in my office."

"You could have told her that I had come to ask your opinion on a professional matter."

Parendon's face expressed mild surprise.

"Would Madame Maigret be satisfied with an explanation like that?"

"My wife never asks questions."

"Mine does. And she goes on asking, just as you do in your interrogations, if one can believe what one reads, until she thinks she has got to the bottom of things. Then she checks on them with seemingly harmless questions which she shoots at Ferdinand, at the cook, at my secretary, at the children. . . ."

He was not complaining. There was no bitterness in his voice. More a kind of admiration, in fact. He seemed to be talking about a phenomenon whose merits are widely known.

"What was her reaction?"

"That it must be revenge on the part of one of the domestics."

"Have they any grounds for complaint?"

"They always have grounds for complaint. For example, Madame Vauquin, the cook, works late when we give a dinner, and the cleaning woman leaves at six sharp, regardless. On the other hand, the cleaning woman earns two hundred francs less than the cook. You understand?"

"What about Ferdinand?"

"Did you know that Ferdinand, who is so correct, so formal, was in the Foreign Legion and has taken part in commando raids? No one checks on what he does in the evenings in his room above the garage, whom he sees or where he goes. . . "

"Are they the people you suspect too?"

The lawyer hesitated a second and decided to be honest. "No."

"Why?"

"None of them would have written the sentences in the letter, or used certain of the words."

"Are there any guns in the house?"

"My wife has two shotguns, because she is often invited on a shoot. I don't shoot."

"I have an old Browning in a drawer of my bedside
"Have you a revolver?"
table. Lots of people do, I think. One tells oneself that if burglars . . ."

He laughed softly.

"I could give them a fright, anyway. Here . . ."

He opened a drawer of the desk and took out a box of cartridges.

"The gun is in my room at the other end of the apartment, and the cartridges are here, a habit I got into when the children were younger and I was afraid of accidents. This makes me realize that they're now well into the age of reason and I could load my Browning. . . ."

He kept on rummaging in the drawer, and this time he pulled out an American-style blackjack.

"Do you know where I got this toy? Three years ago, I was surprised to be called to the police station to see the superintendent. When I got there I was asked if I had a son called Jacques. He was twelve at the time.

"A fight had broken out as the boys were coming out of school, and the policemen found Gus in possession of this blackjack. . . .

"I questioned him when I got home and learned that he had got it from a friend in exchange for six packages of chewing gum."

He smiled, amused at the memory.

"Is he a violent boy?"

"He went through a difficult period when he was between twelve and thirteen. He used to have violent but short-lived tempers, especially when his sister teased him. After that it wore off. I would say he's too calm, too solitary a boy for my liking. . . ."

"Hasn't he any friends?"

"I only know of one, a boy called Génuvier who comes quite often to listen to music with him. His father is a *pâtissier* on Rue du Faubourg-Saint-Honoré—you must have heard the name—ladies go there from all over town. . . ."

"If you will excuse me now, I'll go back to your secretary."

"What do you think of her?"

"She is intelligent, both spontaneous and thoughtful. . . ."

That seemed to please Parendon, who purred:

"I find her invaluable. . . ."

While Parendon immersed himself in his papers once again, Maigret rejoined Mademoiselle Vague in her office. She was not even pretending to work and was obviously waiting for him.

"One question that you will find ridiculous, Mademoiselle—has the Parendon boy . . ."

"Everyone calls him Gus."

"Right. Has Gus ever tried to make love to you?"

"He's fifteen years old."

"I know. That's just the age to be curious about certain things, or for sentimental attachments."

She thought for a moment. Like Parendon, she took time to think before answering. It was as if he had taught her exactitude.

"No," she said finally. "When I first knew him, he was a little boy who came in to ask me for stamps for his collection, a boy who scrounged incredible amounts of pencils and scotch tape. And sometimes he asked me to help him with his homework. He would sit where you are and watch me with a serious expression. . . ."

"And now?"

"He is half a head taller than I am and he has been shaving for a year. If he scrounges anything from me now, it's cigarettes, when he has forgotten to buy any."

She lit one suddenly, while Maigret filled his pipe slowly.

"Aren't his visits any more frequent?"

"Quite the opposite. I think I told you he leads his own life, apart from the family, except for meals. And he even refuses to appear at table when there are guests. He prefers to eat in the kitchen."

"Does he get on well with the staff?"

"He doesn't make any distinctions between people.

49

Even if he is late, he won't let the chauffeur drive him to school, in case the other boys see him in a limousine."

"In fact, he is ashamed of living in a house like this?"

"It's a bit like that, yes."

"Has his relationship with his sister improved?"

"You must remember that I never have meals with them and that I rarely see them together. As far as I can see, he thinks of her as a curious creature and tries to understand how she works, rather the way he would think of an insect."

"What about his mother?"

"She's a bit flamboyant for him. I mean she is always on the move, always talking to a crowd of people. . . ."

"I understand. And the girl? Paulette, I think her name is."

"Everyone here says Bambi. Don't forget that both children have nicknames. Gus and Bambi. I don't know what they call me among themselves—it should be quite funny."

"How does Bambi get on with her mother?"

"Badly."

"Do they quarrel?"

"Not even that. They hardly speak to each other."

"On whose side is the animosity?"

"On Bambi's. You'll be seeing her. Although she's young, she passes judgment on everyone around her, and you can tell by her look that she is judging them cruelly."

"Unjustly?"

"Not always."

"Does she get on with you?"

"She accepts me."

"Does she ever come to see you in your office?"

"When she needs me to type a lecture or photocopy a document."

"Does she ever talk to you about her friends?"

"Never."

"Do you think that she knows about your relationship with her father?"

"I've sometimes wondered about that. I don't know. Anyone could have looked in on us without our knowing."

"Does she love her father?"

"She has taken him under her protection. She seems to think of him as her mother's victim, and that is why she hates her for taking so much of the limelight."

"In fact Monsieur Parendon doesn't play an important role in the family, does he?"

"Not an obvious role."

"Has he never tried?"

"Perhaps he did a long time ago, before I came. He must have seen that the battle was already lost and . . ."

". . . and he retreated into his shell."

She laughed.

"Not as much as you may think. He knows everything that goes on, too. He doesn't ask questions like Madame Parendon—he contents himself with listening, observing, deducing. . . . He is an extremely intelligent man."

"I had that impression."

He saw that she was delighted. Suddenly she looked on him as a friend, as if he had won her over. He realized that if she and Parendon made love it was not because he was her boss, but because she felt a real passion for him.

"I imagine you don't have a lover. . . ."

"That's right. I don't want one."

"Don't you mind living alone?"

"On the contrary. I would find it unbearable to have someone around all the time. Even more so to have someone in my bed."

"No passing affairs?"

Still that slight hesitation between the truth and a lie.

"Sometimes. Very rarely."

And, with a pride that was quite comical, she added as if she were making a profession of faith:

"But never in my apartment."

"What kind of relationship is there between Gus and his father? I did ask before, but we got sidetracked."

"Gus admires him. But he admires him from a distance, without letting him see it, with a kind of humility. You see, to understand them you would have to know the whole family, and your investigations would have to go on forever. . . .

"You know that the apartment belonged to Monsieur Gassin de Beaulieu, and it's full of reminders of him. The former President has been ill for three years and never leaves his house in the Vendée. But before that he sometimes came to spend a week or two here—he still has a room—and from the moment he came in he was master of the house again."

"So you knew him?"

"Very well. He used to dictate all his letters to me."

"What kind of man is he? From his portrait . . ."

"The one in Monsieur Parendon's office? If you have seen the portrait, you have seen the man. What is called an upright and honest judge and a cultivated man. You know what I mean? A man who walked around larger than life and who acted as if he had just stepped down from his pedestal.

"While he was here, no one in the apartment was allowed to make any noise. Everyone walked on tiptoe. They whispered. The children, who were younger then than they are now, lived in terror. . . .

"Monsieur Parendon's father, the surgeon, on the other hand . . ."

"Does he still come?"

"Not very often. That's just what I was going to tell you. You will have heard the stories about him, everyone has. He was the son of peasants in Berry, and he always behaved like a peasant. His speech is intentionally rough and colorful, even in his lectures.

"A few years ago he was still a force of nature. Since he lives very near here, on Rue de Miromesnil, he often used to drop in for a visit, just in passing, and the children adored him.

"That didn't please everyone. . . ."

"Particularly Madame Parendon. . . ."

"It's true there was no love lost between them. I don't know anything for sure. The servants have talked about a violent scene between them. At any rate, he doesn't come any more, but his son goes to visit him every two or three days."

"So the Gassins, in fact, have beaten the Parendons."

"More than you think."

The air was blue with smoke from Maigret's pipe and Mademoiselle Vague's cigarettes. The girl walked over to the window, which she opened wider to let in the fresh air.

"Because," she went on in an amused tone, "the children have aunts, uncles, and cousins. Monsieur Gassin de Beaulieu had four daughters, and the other three live in Paris too. They have children ranging in age from ten to twenty-two. In fact, last spring one of the girls married an officer attached to the Naval Ministry.

"So much for the Gassin de Beaulieu clan. If you'd like it, I'll make up a list for you, with their husbands' names."

"I don't think that will be necessary just now. Do they often come here?"

"Sometimes one of them, sometimes another. Although they've been married for a long time, they still consider this house the family home."

"While on the other hand . . ."

"You have understood what I was going to say before I said it. Monsieur Parendon's brother, Germain, is a doctor, a specialist in infantile neurology. He is married to a former actress who still looks young and vivacious. . . ."

"Does he look like . . . ?"

Maigret was a little embarrassed by his question, and she understood.

"No. He's just as broad and powerful as his father, and much taller. He is an extremely handsome man, and it's surprising to find he's so gentle. He and his wife have no children. They don't go out much and only entertain close friends. . . ."

"But they don't come here," sighed Maigret, who was beginning to form a fairly accurate picture of the family.

"Monsieur Parendon goes to see them on the evenings when his wife plays bridge, since he loathes cards. Sometimes Monsieur Germain comes to visit him in his office. I can tell if he has been when I come in in the morning because the room smells of cigars."

Maigret seemed suddenly to change his tone of voice. He did not grow menacing or severe, but there was no longer a trace of badinage and amusement in his voice and in his eyes.

"Listen to me, Mademoiselle Vague. I am sure you have answered me with complete honesty, and sometimes you have even anticipated my questions. I still have one more to ask you, and I beg you to be just as sincere. Do you think these letters are a joke?"

She answered without hesitation:

"No."

"Before they were written, had you ever felt that something terrible was about to take place in this house?"

This time she hesitated, lit another cigarette, then said:

"Perhaps. . . ."

"When?"

"I don't know. I'm thinking. . . . Perhaps after the summer holidays. Around that time, anyway."

"What did you notice?"

"Nothing in particular. Just something in the air. . . . I'm tempted to say a sort of oppression."

"Who, in your opinion, is the person who is being threatened?"

She blushed suddenly and was silent.

"Why won't you answer?"

"Because you know perfectly well what I would say: Monsieur Parendon."

He stood up, sighing.

"Thank you. I think I have tormented you enough this morning. I'll probably come back to see you again soon."

"Do you want to question the others?"

"Not before lunch. It's almost noon. I expect I'll see them after."

She watched him leave, tall, bulky, awkward, then suddenly, when the front door had closed again, she began to cry.

3

There was a dark little restaurant on **Rue de Miro-mesnil**, a relic of former days, where the **menu** was still written on a slate and where one could see the proprietor's wife through a glass door, a big woman with legs like columns, standing over her stove.

Each of the regulars had his napkin in a pigeonhole and frowned when someone took his seat. That was a rare occurrence since the waitress, Emma, didn't like new faces. Some of the older inspectors from the Rue des Saussaies went there regularly, and so did clerks of the type one hardly ever sees any more, the type one imagines seated in front of ancient black desks, wearing oversleeves.

The proprietor, seated at his desk, recognized the superintendent and came over to welcome him.

"It's a long time since we've seen you around here. Anyway, you can congratulate yourself on your sense of smell —there are andouillettes today."

Maigret liked to eat alone this way from time to time, letting his eye wander over an old-fashioned décor, over characters who for the most part worked in rear courtyards with unexpected offices—disputed-claims offices, security-loans offices, orthopedists, lumber dealers. . . .

As he himself said, he ruminated. He didn't think. His mind wandered from one idea to another, sometimes tying in old cases with the one on hand.

Parendon fascinated him. In his mind, as he ate the crisp, juicy andouillette served with French fries that didn't taste of grease, the gnome assumed aspects which were both moving and frightening.

"Article 64, Monsieur Maigret! Don't forget Article 64!"

Was it really an obsession with him? Why did this important lawyer, whom people came from all over the world to consult at great expense on maritime matters, why did he so hypnotize himself with the article of the Penal Code which in fact dealt with human responsibility?

Oh, yes, he did it prudently. Without giving the slightest definition of dementia. And limiting it to the moment of the action, that is to say, to the moment of the actual crime.

He knew some psychiatrists of the old school, the men the judges like to choose as experts because they do not look for subtleties. Those men, in delimiting the responsibility of a criminal, only take lesions and other abnormalities of the brain into account, or, since the Penal Code mentions it in the next article, epilepsy.

But how can one establish that a man, at the moment when he killed another, at the precise moment of the death blow, was in full possession of his faculites? How, even more important, can one swear that he was capable of resisting the impulse?

Article 64, yes . . . Maigret had often argued about it, particularly with his old friend Pardon. It was argued over, too, at almost every congress of the International Society of Criminology, and there were fat volumes on the subject, the very volumes which filled a large part of Parendon's library.

"Well? Is it good?"

The jovial proprietor refilled his glass with a Beaujolais which was perhaps on the young side but had exactly the right fruity taste.

"Your wife hasn't lost her touch."

"She'd be pleased if you would go and tell her that before you leave."

The apartment was the very image of a man like Gassin de Beaulieu, a man of authority, a Commander of the Legion of Honor, a man who had never had any doubts about the Code, about the law, or about himself.

Seated at the tables around Maigret were thin men, fat men, men in their thirties, men in their fifties. Almost all of them were eating alone, staring into space or at a newspaper. They had in common that particular patina given by a humble, monotonous way of life.

There is a tendency to imagine people the way one wishes them to be. Here, one man had a crooked nose or a receding chin, another had one shoulder too low, while his neighbor was obese. Half of the heads were bald, and more than half of those eating wore glasses.

Why did Maigret think of that? For no reason in particular. Because Parendon, in his huge study, looked like a gnome; others, more cruel, might have said like a monkey.

As for Madame Parendon . . . He had hardly seen her. She had only put in a rapid appearance, as if to give him a sample of her brilliant personality. How had that pair got together? By what happy meeting or through what clever stroke of family business?

And there was also Gus, who worked at his hi-fi and electronics in his bedroom with the *pâtissier*'s son. He was taller, stronger than his father, luckily, and, if one could believe Mademoiselle Vague, he was a well-balanced boy.

There was also his sister Bambi, studying archaeology. Did she really intend to dig in the deserts of the Near East someday, or were those studies only a blind?

Mademoiselle Vague fiercely defended her employer, with whom she could only make love in the corner of the office, on the sly.

Why in heaven's name didn't they meet somewhere else? Were they both so afraid of Madame Parendon? Or was it through a sense of guilt that they had to keep the furtive, impromptu element in their relationship?

There were also the former legionnaire turned butler, the cook and the housekeeper who detested each other because of their hours of work and their wages. And a maid called Lise whom Maigret hadn't yet met and who had scarcely been mentioned to him.

There was René Tortu, who had slept just once with the secretary and was at present dragging out a long engagement to another girl. Finally there was Julien Baud, who was learning about Paris as a lawyer's copying clerk before breaking into the world of the theater.

Whose side were they on, each of them? The Gassins'? The Parendons'?

Someone in that list wanted to kill someone else.

And—an ironic touch—a former inspector of Criminal Investigation held the post of concierge downstairs.

The gardens of the President of the Republic were across the street and, through the trees which were beginning to turn green, although it was early yet, the well-known steps where he was photographed shaking hands with his important guests.

Wasn't there a certain lack of cohesion? The bistrot, the things around Maigret, seemed more real, more solid. It was everyday life. Unimportant people, yes, but there are more unimportant people than there are others, even if they are less often noticed, dress soberly, speak more quietly, hug the walls as they walk along or crowd together in the métro.

He was automatically served a *baba au rhum* liberally covered with whipped cream, another of the proprietor's wife's specialties. Maigret remembered to go into the kitchen to shake hands with her. He even had to kiss her on both cheeks. It was the tradition.

"I hope it won't be so long before you come again."

If the murderer took his time, Maigret might well be back often. . . .

For his thoughts kept returning to the murderer. To the murderer who was not yet a murderer. To the potential murderer.

Are there not thousands and thousands of potential murderers in Paris?

Why had this one felt it necessary to warn Maigret in advance? Through a kind of romanticism? To make himself interesting? Or did he want to be stopped before he did anything?

How could he be stopped?

Maigret walked up as far as Saint-Philippe-du-Roule in the sunshine and turned to the left, stopping from time to time in front of a shop window: very expensive things, often quite useless, which people bought anyway.

He passed the Papeterie Roman, where he amused himself by reading names straight out of the Almanach de Gotha on visiting cards or engraved invitations. This was where the paper that had started it all had come from. Without the anonymous letters, Maigret might still not have known the Parendons, the Gassin de Beaulieus, the aunts, the uncles, the cousins.

Like him, other people were walking along the sidewalks just for the pleasure of blinking in the sunlight and breathing the air with its little gusts of warmth. He felt like shrugging his shoulders, jumping on the first open bus that came along, and going back to the Quai.

"To hell with the Parendons!"

Back there he might find some poor devil who had really killed, because for him that was the only way out, or perhaps a young tough from Pigalle, newly arrived from

Marseilles or Bastia, who had done in a rival to prove he was a man.

He took a seat on a café terrace, near a stove, to drink his coffee. Then he went inside and shut himself in the telephone booth.

"This is Maigret. Get me someone from my office, please. . . . It doesn't matter. Janvier, Lucas, or Lapointe if you can. . . ."

It was Lapointe who answered.

"Anything new, son?"

"A phone call from Madame Parendon. She wanted to speak to you yourself, and I had a terrible time getting her to understand that you have lunch just like anyone else. . . ."

"What did she want?"

"She wants you to go and see her as soon as possible."

"At home?"

"Yes. She'll wait for you until four o'clock. She has an important appointment after that."

"With her hairdresser, no doubt. Is that all?"

"No, but the other might be a joke. . . . Half an hour ago the switchboard girl had someone on the line, a man or a woman, she couldn't tell which, an odd voice, or it might have been a child's. . . . Anyway, the person was breathing hard, in a hurry or upset, and he said very quickly:

" 'Tell Superintendent Maigret to hurry. . . .'

"The girl had no time to ask anything—the person had already hung up.

"It isn't a letter this time, and that's why I'm asking myself . . ."

Maigret almost told him:

"Don't ask yourself anything."

He wasn't asking himself any questions. He wasn't trying to play guessing games, but that didn't stop him from being worried.

"Thank you, son. I'm just going back to Avenue Marigny. If anything comes up, you can call me there."

The fingerprints on the two letters hadn't been of any use. For years incriminating fingerprints have been getting rarer and rarer because they have been talked about so much in the papers, in novels, and on television that even the most obtuse criminals take precautions.

He walked past the lodge where the former inspector from the Rue des Saussaies greeted him with respectful familiarity. The Rolls stood in front of the porch, with no one in it except the chauffeur. Maigret climbed up to the first floor and rang the bell.

"Good afternoon, Ferdinand."

He was becoming a part of the household, wasn't he?

"I'll take you to Madame. . . ."

Ferdinand had had his instructions. She had left nothing to chance. His hat was taken away as if he were in a restaurant, and for the first time he walked through an immense drawing room such as a Minister of State might have. There were no personal objects lying around—no scarf, no cigarette holder, no open book. Not a speck in the ashtrays. Three tall, open windows looked out on the quiet courtyard, which was now bathed in sunshine and where no cars were being washed.

A hall. A sharp turn. The apartment seemed to consist of a central body and two wings, like an old château. A strip of red carpeting ran on the white marble floor. Always the too high ceilings, which dwarfed everyone.

Ferdinand knocked gently at a double door, which he opened without waiting for a reply, and announced:

"Superintendent Maigret."

He found himself in an empty boudoir, but Madame Parendon appeared immediately from a neighboring room, her arm outstretched, walking up to Maigret, whose hand she shook vigorously.

"I am a little ashamed, Superintendent, of having telephoned you, or rather of having telephoned one of your subordinates. . . ."

Here everything was blue: the silk brocade covering the walls, the Louis XV armchairs, the upholstery; even the yellow-patterned Chinese carpet had a blue background.

Was it by chance that, at two in the afternoon, she was still wearing à housecoat, an elegant turquoise-blue housecoat?

"Forgive me for receiving you in my den, as I call it, but it is the only place where one isn't constantly interrupted. . . ."

The door through which she had come was still ajar, and he caught a glimpse of a dressing table, also Louis XV, which indicated that it was her bedroom.

"Do sit down."

She pointed to a fragile chair into which the superintendent eased himself carefully, telling himself not to move too much.

"Do smoke your pipe. . . ."

Even if he didn't want to! She wanted him to be like the newspaper photographs. The photographers, too, never failed to remind him:

"Your pipe, Superintendent . . ."

As if he puffed at his pipe from morning till night! What if he wanted to smoke a cigarette? Or a cigar? Or not smoke at all?

He did not like the chair he was sitting in, which he expected to collapse at any moment. He did not like this blue boudoir or this woman in blue who was giving him a veiled smile.

She was sitting in an easy chair. She lit a cigarette with a gold lighter such as he had seen in Cartier's window. The cigarette case was gold. Quite a few things in these rooms must be gold.

"I am a little jealous of the fact that you went to see the little Vague girl before you came to see me. This morning . . ."

"I shouldn't have dared to disturb you so early. . . ."

Was he going to turn into a diplomatic Maigret? He was annoyed at his own suavity.

"No doubt you have been told that I get up late and that I keep to my rooms until midday. . . . It is true and it isn't. I lead a very busy life, Monsieur Maigret, and in fact I start my days early.

"First of all, there is this big house to run. If I didn't

telephone to the shops myself, I don't know what we should eat, nor what kind of bills we should get at the end of the month. Madame Vauquin is an excellent cook, but the telephone still frightens her and makes her stammer. The children take up my time. Even though they are grown up now, I have to take an interest in their clothes, their activities. . . .

"If it weren't for me, Gus would live in jeans, a sweater, and tennis shoes all year round. . . .

"It doesn't matter. I won't mention the charity work I am involved in. Other people are content to send a check or to attend a cocktail party, but when it's a question of real work, you won't find anyone . . ."

He waited patiently, politely, so patiently and so politely that he did not bring her back to the matter in hand.

"I imagine you lead a very busy life too."

"You understand, Madame, I am only a civil servant."

She laughed, showing all her teeth, the tip of a pink tongue. Her tongue was very pointed, he noticed. She was blonde, almost a strawberry blonde, and her eyes were the color usually called green, but which is more often a dark gray.

Was she forty? A bit more? A bit less? Forty-five? It was impossible to say, such was the effect of the beautician's work.

"I must tell that to Jacqueline. . . . She is the wife of the Minister of the Interior, one of my best friends. . . ."

Good! He had been warned. She had wasted no time in playing her first trump.

"I may appear to be joking. . . . I am joking. . . . But

67

you must realize that that is only a front. In fact, Monsieur Maigret, I am tormented by what is happening, more than tormented . . ."

Then, straight to the point:

"What did you think of my husband?"

"He is very pleasant. . . ."

"Of course. That's what everyone says. I mean . . ."

"He is very intelligent, remarkably intelligent."

She was growing impatient. She knew what she was getting at and he was interrupting her. Maigret, looking at her hands, noted that they were older than her face.

"I think that he is very sensitive, too."

"If you were being quite honest, wouldn't you say he is oversensitive?"

He opened his mouth to reply, but this time it was she who won, adding:

"Sometimes he frightens me, he is so introspective. He is a man who suffers. I have always known that. When I married him there was a certain amount of pity in my love for him."

Maigret played the idiot.

"Why?"

For a moment she was put out of her stride.

"But . . . but you have seen him. Right from childhood, he must have been ashamed of his looks."

"He isn't tall. Many other men . . ."

"Look here, Superintendent." She braced herself. "Let us lay our cards on the table. I don't know what his heredity is, or rather I know only too well. His mother was a young nurse at Laënnec, a ward maid really, and she was only sixteen when Professor Parendon got her with child. Why on earth, since he was a surgeon, didn't he do an abortion? Did she threaten to expose him? I don't know. . . . What I do know is that Emile was a seven-months baby. . . . That is, a premature baby."

"Most premature babies grow into normal children. . . ."

"Do you think he is normal?"

"In what sense?"

She stubbed her cigarette out nervously, only to light another.

"Excuse me. You seem to be avoiding the issue, to be trying not to understand."

"To understand what?"

She couldn't stand it any longer, got up suddenly, and began to pace the Chinese rug.

"To understand why I am worried, why, as they say, I am all worked up. For almost twenty years I have forced myself to protect him, to make him happy, to give him a normal life. . . ."

He kept on smoking his pipe in silence, his eyes following her. She was wearing extremely elegant slippers which must have been made to measure.

"Those letters he told me about . . . I don't know who wrote them, but they reflect my own fears quite closely."

"Has this been going on for a long time?"

"Weeks . . . Months . . . I hardly dare say years. When we were first married we went out together, we went to the theater, we dined in town . . ."

"Did that make him happy?"

"It relaxed him, at any rate. I suspect now that he never feels at ease, that he is ashamed that he is not like other men, that he has always felt that way. . . .

"Wait! Even his choice of Maritime Law as a career . . . Can you tell me for what reason a man like him could have chosen Maritime Law? It was a sort of act of defiance. Since he couldn't plead at assizes . . ."

"Why not?"

She looked at him helplessly.

"Well really, Monsieur Maigret, you know that as well as I do. Can you see that pale, insignificant little man in the great hall of the assizes, defending a criminal's life?"

He decided not to tell her in turn that one noted barrister of the previous century was only four feet three.

"He is bored. As time goes on, as he grows older, he shuts himself away more and more, and when we have a dinner party I have a dreadful time to get him to be present. . . ."

He also refrained from asking her who made up the guest list.

He listened, and he watched.

He watched and tried not to worry, because the picture this taut-nerved woman with her burning energy was painting of her husband was both true and false.

True in what respect?

False in what respect?

That was what he would have liked to unravel. His vision of Emile Parendon was becoming like a blurred photograph. The contours were not clear. The features changed expression according to the angle from which they were viewed.

It was true that he was enclosed in a world of his own, the world, one might say, of Article 64. Was he a responsible person? An irresponsible one? Other men besides him were passionately interested in that most important question, and councils had argued over it since the Middle Ages.

In his case, had the thought not become an obsession? Maigret remembered his own entry into the study the previous day, and the look which Parendon had shot at him, as if the superintendent was for him at that moment a sort of incarnation of the celebrated article or was capable of giving him an answer to it.

The lawyer had not asked him what he had come about, what he wanted. He had spoken of Article 64, his mouth almost trembling with passion.

It was true that . . .

Yes, he did lead an almost solitary life in this house which was as much too big for him as a giant's coat would have been.

How, with his stunted body, with all the thoughts that whirled around in his head, did he face this woman daily —this woman who was so nervous that her nervousness was communicated to everything around her?

It was true that . . .

A half-pint, maybe. A gnome—that too, perhaps.

But sometimes, when the neighboring rooms appeared to be empty, when the time seemed right, he made love to Mademoiselle Vague.

What was true? What was false? Didn't even Bambi protect herself from her mother by taking refuge in archaeology?

"Listen to me, Monsieur Maigret. I am not the empty-headed woman you may have been told about. I am a woman with specific responsibilities—a woman, moreover, who makes a great effort to lead a useful life. Our father brought us up that way, my sisters and me. He was a man of duty. . . ."

Oh, oh! The superintendent did not like the sound of those words: the righteous judge, the pride of the Bench, teaching his daughters the sense of duty. . . .

With her, however, it rang a little false. She did not give her mind time to fasten itself on to a sentence, for her face, her whole body, quivered and word succeeded word, idea followed idea, images changed in quick succession.

"There is fear in this house, that is true. . . . And I am the one who feels that fear most. . . . No! You mustn't believe that I wrote those letters. . . . I am too direct to use such devious methods. . . .

"If I had wanted to see you I would have telephoned you, as I did this morning. . . .

"I am afraid—not so much for me, but for him. . . . I don't know what he might do, but I feel he may do something, that he has reached the brink, that a sort of demon inside him is impelling him to take some dramatic action. . . ."

"What makes you think that?"

"You have seen him, haven't you?"

"He seemed to me to be very calm and well balanced, and I found he had a well-developed sense of humor."

"An irritating sense of humor, not to say a black one. . . . That man is consuming himself. His work only takes up two or three days a week, and the greater part of his research is done by René Tortu. . . .

"He reads journals, writes letters to all parts of the world, to people he has never met but whose articles he has read.

"He often spends days at a time without setting foot outside, happy just to watch the world go by through the windows . . . Always the same chestnut trees, the same wall around the gardens of the Elysée Palace. . . . I nearly said even the same people going by. . . .

"You have come here twice, and you have not asked to see me. . . . But unfortunately I am the most interested party. . . . I am his wife, do not forget that, even if he seems to forget it sometimes. . . . We have two children who still need to be taken care of. . . ."

She gave him a moment's breathing space when she lit a cigarette. It was the fourth. She smoked greedily, without slowing her rate of speech, and the boudoir was already filled with clouds of smoke.

"I don't think that you can foresee any better than I can what he will do. . . . Would he take his own life? It is possible, and I would be very upset after having tried for so many years to make him happy. . . .

"Is it my fault if I haven't succeeded?

"Perhaps I shall be the victim, which is more likely, because he has come to hate me, little by little. . . . Can you understand that? His brother, who is a neurologist, could explain. . . . He needs to project his disillusionment, his bitterness, his humiliations on to someone. . . ."

"Excuse me if . . ."

"Let me finish, please. Tomorrow, the next day, someday, you will perhaps be called here and you will find yourself in front of a dead woman who will be me. . . .

"I forgive him in advance, because I know he is not responsible and that medicine, in spite of all its progress . . ."

"Do you consider your husband to be a medical case?"

She looked at him with a kind of defiance.

"Yes."

"A mental case?"

"Perhaps."

"Have you consulted any doctors?"

"Yes."

"Doctors who know him?"

"We have several doctors among our friends."

"What exactly have they told you?"

"To take care . . ."

"To take care of what?"

"We haven't gone into details. They were not consultations, but social conversations."

"Are they all of the same opinion?"

"Several of them are."

"Can you give me their names?"

Maigret said that so that he could take his black notebook out of his pocket. The gesture was enough to make her beat a retreat.

"It wouldn't be right to give you their names, but if you want to have him examined by an expert . . ."

Maigret had put aside his patient, bland manner. His face too was strained, for things were beginning to happen quickly.

"When you telephoned my office to ask me to come to see you, did you already have that in mind?"

"Have what in mind?"

"To ask me more or less directly to have your husband examined by a psychiatrist."

"Did I say that? That is a word I never even mentioned."

"But the thought showed clearly behind everything you said. . . ."

"In that case either you have misunderstood me or I have expressed myself badly. Perhaps I am too frank, too spontaneous. . . . I don't take the trouble to choose my words. . . . What I said to you, what I am repeating now, is that I am afraid, that there is fear running loose in this house. . . ."

"And I am repeating to you, fear of what?"

She sat down again as if she were exhausted, and looked at him hopelessly.

"I don't know what I can say to you now, Superintendent. I thought you would understand without my having to go into details. I am afraid for myself, for him. . . ."

"In other words, you are afraid that he may kill you or that he may commit suicide?"

"Put that way, it seems ridiculous, I know, when everything around us is so peaceful."

"Forgive me if I seem indiscreet. Does your husband still have sexual relations with you?"

"Up until a year ago . . ."

"What happened a year ago to change the situation?"

"I came upon him with that girl. . . ."

"Mademoiselle Vague?"

"Yes."

"In the office?"

"It was so sordid. . . ."

"And after that you shut your door to him? Did he ever try to come in?"

"Only once. I told him what my reasons were and he understood."

"Didn't he insist?"

"He didn't even apologize. He went away just like someone who has got out at the wrong floor."

"Have you had any lovers?"

"What?"

Her eyes had grown hard, her look sharp and spiteful.

"I am asking you," he repeated calmly, "if you have had any lovers. These things happen, don't they?"

"Not in our family, Superintendent, and if my father were here . . ."

"In his capacity as judge, your father would understand that it is my duty to ask you the question. You have just spoken to me of an atmosphere of fear, of a threat hanging over you and your husband. You suggest, in veiled terms, that I should have him examined by a psychiatrist. So it is natural . . ."

"Forgive me. I let myself get carried away. No, I have not had any lovers, and I never shall have."

"Do you have a gun?"

She got up, walked quickly to the neighboring room, returned, and handed Maigret a small mother-of-pearl-handled revolver.

"Be careful. It's loaded."

"Have you had it long?"

"One of my friends, a woman with a really black sense of humor, gave it to me when I got married."

"Aren't you afraid that the children, playing around . . . ?"

"They rarely come into my bedroom, and when they were younger this gun was kept in a locked drawer."

"Your shotguns?"

"They are in a case and the case is in the coach house, with our trunks, suitcases, and golf bags."

"Does your husband play golf?"

"I've tried to get him interested, but he gets out of breath by the third hole."

"Is he often ill?"

"He has few serious illnesses. The worst, if I remember rightly, was an attack of pleurisy. On the other hand, he is constantly afflicted by little things, laryngitis, influenza, head colds . . ."

"Does he call in his doctor?"

"Of course."

"One of your friends?"

"No. A doctor from nearby, Dr. Martin, who lives on Rue du Cirque, the street behind this one."

"Has Dr. Martin ever spoken to you privately?"

"No, he hasn't, but I have often waited to catch him as he left, to make sure that my husband had nothing serious."

"What did he say?"

"He said no. . . . That men like him often live the longest. He told me about Voltaire, who . . ."

"I know about Voltaire. Has he ever suggested that your husband consult a specialist?"

"No. . . . Only . . ."

"Only what?"

"What's the use? You will only misinterpret my words again."

"Try, anyway."

"I can tell from your attitude that my husband has made an excellent impression on you, and I was sure that that would be the case. I won't say that he plays a part consciously. With strangers, he is a lively man, making a great show of stability. With Dr. Martin, he speaks and acts as he does with you. . . ."

"And with the servants?"

"He is not responsible for the work of the domestics."

"What does that mean?"

"That he does not have to reprimand them. He leaves that task to me, so that I have to do the dirty work. . . ."

Maigret was stifling in the oversoft chair, in the boudoir whose blue was becoming unbearable to him. He got up and nearly stretched himself as he would have done in his own office.

"Have you anything else to tell me?"

She too stood up and measured him as one equal with another.

"There would be no point."

"Do you want me to send an inspector to keep permanent watch in the apartment?"

"The idea is quite ridiculous."

"Not if I am to believe your premonitions."

"It is not a question of premonitions."

"It is not a question of facts, either."

"Not yet. . . ."

"Let us recap. . . . For some time, your husband has been showing signs of mental derangement. . . ."

"That's it exactly!"

"He withdraws into himself and his behavior worries you. . . ."

"That is nearer the truth."

"You are afraid for his life or for yours. . . ."

"I admit that."

"Which one do you think it will be?"

"If I knew that. I would be slightly less worried.'

"Someone living in this house, or someone who has easy access to it, sent us at the Quai two letters announcing that a murder would take place shortly. I may add, now, that there has also been a telephone call in my absence. . . ."

"Why didn't you tell me about that?"

"Because I was listening to you. This message, a very brief one, only confirms the ones that preceded it. The unknown man or woman said, more or less, 'Tell Superintendent Maigret it will be soon. . . .'"

He watched her grow pale. She was not acting. Her face suddenly became lifeless, except for patches of rouge. The corners of her lips collapsed.

"Oh! . . ."

She lowered her head, and her thin body seemed to have lost its prodigious energy.

At that moment he forgot his annoyance and pitied her.

"Do you still not want me to send you someone?"

"What good would that do?"

"What do you mean?"

"If something is going to happen, the presence of a policeman who will be stationed heaven knows where won't stop it. . . ."

"Do you know that your husband has an automatic?"

"Yes."

"Does he know that you have this revolver?"

"Of course."

"And your children?"

Her nerves so taut that she was almost weeping, she cried:

"My children have nothing to do with this, can't you understand that? They mind their own business and not ours. They have their own lives to live. They laugh at ours, what there is left of it. . . ."

She had spoken vehemently again, as if certain subjects unleashed her anger automatically.

"You may go now! Forgive me for not showing you out. I don't know what I expected. . . . Whatever is going to happen, let it happen! . . . Go and see my husband, or that girl. . . . Good-by, Monsieur Maigret. . . ."

She had opened the door for him, waited until he was gone and shut it again. Already, in the corridor, it seemed to the superintendent that he had come out of another world, and the blue of the boudoir he had just left haunted him still.

He looked out through a window into the yard where a different chauffeur from the one in the morning was polishing a different car. It was still sunny, with a light breeze.

He was tempted to take his hat from the cloakroom, since he knew where it was, and to leave without saying anything. Then, as if in spite of himself, he went to Mademoiselle Vague's office.

She was wearing a white smock over her dress and was photocopying documents. The venetian blinds were closed, letting in only a few rays of light.

"Do you want to see Monsieur Parendon?"

"No."

"That's just as well, because he's in conference with two important clients. One of them has come from Amsterdam and the other from Athens. They are both shipowners who . . ."

He wasn't listening, and she went to open the venetian blinds, flooding the narrow room with sunshine.

"You look tired."

"I've spent an hour with Madame Parendon."

"I know."

He looked at the switchboard.

81

"Did you put through her call to the Quai des Orfèvres?"

"No. I didn't even know she had phoned. It was Lise who told me when she came in and asked me for a stamp. . . ."

"Who is Lise?"

"Her maid."

"I know. I mean what kind of person is she?"

"An ordinary girl, like me. We are both from the provinces. I'm from a small town and she's from the country. Since I had some education, I became a secretary, and since she hadn't, she became a maid. . . ."

"How old is she?"

"Twenty-three. I know how old everyone is, because I fill out the forms for Social Security."

"Is she a devoted servant?"

"She does what she is told to do very conscientiously, and I don't think she has any desire to change her job."

"Has she any lovers?"

"When she has her day off, Saturday . . ."

"Is she intelligent enough to have written the letters you have read?"

"Certainly not."

"Did you know that Madame Parendon came upon you with her husband about a year ago?"

"I told you that it had happened once, but there have been other times when she could have opened and shut the door again without being heard. . . ."

"Has Parendon told you that his wife has refused to have sexual relations with him since then?"

"They were very infrequent anyway."

"Why?"

"Because he doesn't love her."

"Doesn't love her, or doesn't love her any longer?"

"That depends on what you mean by the word 'love.' He was no doubt flattered that she married him and for years he forced himself to show his gratitude. . . ."

Maigret smiled, thinking that on the other side of the wall two important shipowners who had come from the opposite ends of Europe were putting their prosperity into the hands of the little man whom Mademoiselle Vague and he were discussing in such a way.

To them, he was not an odd, half-impotent gnome, closed in on himself, mulling over unhealthy thoughts, but one of the luminaries of Maritime Law. Were the three of them not playing with hundreds of millions while Madame Parendon, furious or depressed, disappointed in any case, dressed for her four o'clock appointment?

"Won't you sit down?"

"I think I'll have a look next door."

"You'll only find Julien Baud there. Tortu is at the Law Courts."

He gestured vaguely.

"Well, Julien Baud, then."

4

It seemed to Maigret as if he had gone into another apartment. Just as the rest of the house was orderly, mummified in a solemnity previously established by President Gassin de Beaulieu, so in the office René Tortu shared with young Julien Baud disorder and casualness struck one's eye immediately.

By the window, a desk of the kind common to all businesses was covered with reports, and green files were piled on the pine shelving that had been added progressively as it was needed. There were even files on the floor, on the waxed parquet.

As for Julien Baud's desk, it was an old kitchen table covered with wrapping paper fastened with thumbtacks. Photographs of nudes cut out of magazines were attached to the walls with scotch tape. When the superintendent pushed open the door, Baud was sticking stamps on envelopes, which he weighted one by one. He raised his head and looked at him without surprise, without any emotion, appearing to be wondering what Maigret wanted.

"Are you looking for Tortu?"

"No. I know he's at the Law Courts."

"He'll be back before long."

"I'm not looking for him."

"For whom, then?"

"No one in particular."

Julien Baud was a well-built young man with red hair and freckled cheeks. His china-blue eyes reflected absolute calm.

"Would you care to sit down?"

"No."

"As you like. . . ."

He went on weighing the letters, some of which were in large manila envelopes, then he consulted a little booklet giving the postal rates for the different countries.

"Do you find that interesting?" Maigret asked.

"You know, since I first came to Paris . . ."

He had a trace of a delightful accent, drawing out certain syllables.

"Where do you come from?"

"From Morges. . . . On the shore of Lake Geneva. Do you know it?"

"I've been through it. . . ."

"It's lovely, *n'est-ce pas?*"

The *n'est-ce pas* had a special lilt.

"Yes, it is lovely. . . . What do you think of this household?"

He mistook the word "household" for "house."

"It's big. . . ."

"How do you get on with Monsieur Parendon?"

"I don't see him much. In my position I stick on stamps, I go to the post office, I run the errands, I tie up parcels. . . . I'm not very important. From time to time the boss comes into the office and taps me on the shoulder and asks, 'Everything all right, young man?'

"As for the servants, they all call me the little Swiss, even though I'm five foot eleven in my socks."

"Do you get on well with Mademoiselle Vague?"

"She's nice. . . ."

"What do you think of her?"

"Well, you see, she's on the other side of the fence too, the boss's side."

"What do you mean?"

"What I say, of course. They have their work there, and we have ours. When the boss needs someone, it's not me, it's her . . ."

His face had an expression of naïveté, but the superintendent was not sure that it was not a calculated naïveté.

"I understand you want to be a playwright?"

"I try to write plays. I have already written two, but they're bad. When one comes from the canton of Vaud, like me, one has to get used to Paris first. . . ."

"Does Tortu help you?"

"Help me with what?"

"To get to know Paris. By taking you around, for example. . . ."

"He has never taken me anywhere. He has other things to do."

"What?"

"His fiancée, his friends . . . As soon as I got off the train at the Gare de Lyon, I understood. . . . Here, it's everyone for himself."

"Do you often see Madame Parendon?"

"Quite often, especially in the mornings. When she has forgotten to telephone one of the tradesmen, she comes to see me.

" 'My dear Baud, would you be so good as to order a leg of lamb and ask them to send it around at once. If they haven't anyone to send, run around to the butcher's, will you?'

"So I go to the butcher's, to the fish store, to the grocer's. . . . I go to her shoemaker if there's a scratch on a shoe. It's always 'My dear Baud' . . . do this or stick on the stamps. . . ."

"What is your opinion of her?"

"Maybe I'll put her in one of my plays . . ."

"Because she is somewhat out of the ordinary?"

"There's no one quite ordinary here. They're all nuts."

"Your boss too?"

"He's intelligent, that's for sure, because if he wasn't he wouldn't do the job he does, but he's a nut case, isn't he? With all the money he makes he could do something besides staying all the time sitting at his desk or in an armchair. He's not very strong, I know, but still . . ."

"Do you know about his relationship with Mademoiselle Vague?"

"Everyone knows about that. But he could afford to pay

for ten women, for a hundred, if you see what I mean. . . ."

"And his relationship with his wife?"

"What relationship? They live in the same house and meet each other in the hallway like people passing in the street. Once I had to go into the dining room during lunch, because I was alone in the office and there had just been an urgent telegram. . . . Well! They were all sitting there like strangers in a restaurant. . . ."

"You don't seem very fond of them."

"I'm not complaining. They provide characters for me."

"Comic ones?"

"Comic and tragic at the same time. Like life. . . ."

"Have you heard about the letters?"

"Of course."

"Have you any idea who could have written them?"

"It could have been anyone. . . . It could have been me. . . ."

"Did you do it?"

"No. . . . It never occurred to me."

"Does the girl get on well with you?"

"Mademoiselle Bambi?"

He shrugged his shoulders.

"I wonder if she would recognize me in the street. When she needs something, paper, scissors, anything, she comes in and helps herself without saying anything, then she goes away again, still not saying anything."

"Is she a snob?"

"Maybe she isn't. Maybe it's just the way she is."

"Do you believe, too, that something terrible is going to happen?"

He looked at Maigret with his big blue eyes.

"Tragedy can strike anywhere. . . . Listen, last year, one sunny day just like this, a little old lady who was walking along was run over by a bus just outside the house. . . . Well, a few seconds before, she didn't know anything was going to happen. . . ."

There were hurried steps in the hall. A young man of about thirty, brown-haired, tall, stopped short in the doorway. He was carrying a briefcase and had an air of importance about him.

"Superintendent Maigret, I suppose."

"You suppose correctly."

"Did you wish to see me? Have you been waiting for me long?"

"I wasn't waiting for anyone, in fact. . . ."

He was quite handsome, with his dark hair, his well-defined features, his aggressive way of looking at people. One could tell that he was determined to be successful.

"Won't you sit down?" he asked, going over to the desk where he set down his briefcase.

"I've been sitting down a good part of the day. We were just chatting, your young colleague and I. . . ."

The word "colleague" visibly shocked René Tortu, who shot a dirty look at the young Swiss.

"I had an important case at the Law Courts. . . ."

"I know. Do you plead often?"

"Whenever a conciliation becomes impossible. Maître

Parendon rarely appears in person before the judges. We prepare the dossiers and then it is my duty . . ."

"I understand."

The young man had no doubts as to his own importance.

"What do you think of Maître Parendon?"

"As a man or as a jurist?"

"As both."

"As a jurist, he is head and shoulders above his colleagues, and there is no one more able than he to spot the weak point in an adversary's argument."

"And as a man?"

"Working for him, being so to speak his sole assistant, it is not my place to judge him on that basis."

"Do you think he is vulnerable?"

"I would not have thought of that word. Let's say that in his place I would lead a more active life."

"Being present at the receptions given by his wife, for example, going to the theater with her, or dining out?"

"Perhaps. . . . There are other things in life besides books and dossiers."

"Have you read the letters?"

"Maître Parendon has showed me the photostats."

"Do you believe it is a joke?"

"Perhaps. I must confess I haven't thought about it much."

"And yet they announce that something terrible is going to happen imminently, in this house."

Tortu said nothing. He took some papers out of his briefcase and put them in the files.

"Would you marry a girl who was a younger edition of Madame Parendon?"

Tortu looked at him in amazement.

"I'm already engaged, didn't you know? So there's no question . . ."

"It's a way of asking you what you think of her."

"She is active, intelligent, and she knows how to treat . . ."

He looked toward the door suddenly and there, standing in the doorway, was the woman they were talking about. She was wearing a leopard-skin coat over a black silk dress. She was either going out or she had just come in.

"Are you still here?" she asked in astonishment, giving the superintendent a calm, cold look.

"As you can see . . ."

It was difficult to know how long she had been in the hall and how much of the conversation she had heard. Maigret understood what Mademoiselle Vague had meant when she spoke of a house where one never knew if one was being spied on.

"My dear Baud, would you telephone the Comtesse de Prange immediately and tell her that I shall be at least a quarter of an hour late because I was held up at the last moment? . . . Mademoiselle Vague is occupied with my husband and those gentlemen. . . ."

She left, after a last hard look at Maigret. Julien Baud picked up the telephone receiver. As for Tortu, he must have been pleased, because if Madame Parendon had heard his last words she could only be grateful to him.

"Hello. . . . Is this the residence of the Comtesse de Prange?"

Maigret shrugged his shoulders and left. Julien Baud amused him, and he wasn't at all sure that the boy wouldn't make a success of a career as a dramatist. As for Tortu, he did not like him at all, for no reason in particular.

Just as he reached the cloakroom, to get his hat, Ferdinand appeared as if by chance.

"Do you stay near the door all day?"

"No, Superintendent. . . . I only thought it would not be long before you left. . . . Madame went out a few moments ago."

"I know. . . . Have you ever been in jail, Ferdinand?"

"Only military prison, in Africa."

"Are you French?"

"I'm from Aubagne."

"Then why did you enlist in the Foreign Legion?"

"I was young. . . . I had done some stupid things. . . ."

"In Aubagne?"

"In Toulon. Bad company, that sort of thing. . . . When I thought things were about to go badly for me I enlisted in the Legion, saying I was Belgian."

"Have you ever been in trouble since?"

"I've been in service with Monsieur Parendon for eight years, and he has never made any complaint."

"Do you like this job?"

"There are worse. . . ."

"Does Monsieur Parendon treat you well?"

"They don't come any better than him. . . ."

"And Madame?"

"Between you and me, she's a bitch."

"Does she give you a hard time?"

"She gives everyone a hard time. . . . She is everywhere, sticks her nose into everything, complains about everything. . . . Thank God my room is over the garage."

"So that you can have your girl friends in?"

"If I were as foolish as to do that and she found out, she'd fire me on the spot. As far as she's concerned, servants should be castrated. . . . No, but being over there lets me breathe easy. It also allows me to go out when I want, even though there's a bell in my apartment and I'm supposed to be on call, she says, twenty-four hours a day. . . ."

"Has she ever called you at night?"

"Three or four times. Probably just to make sure that I was there."

"What was her excuse?"

"Once, she had heard a suspicious noise and she made a tour of the rooms with me looking for a burglar. . . ."

"Was it a cat?"

"There isn't a cat or dog in the house—she wouldn't stand for it. When Monsieur Gus was younger, he asked for a puppy for Christmas, but he got an electric train instead. I've never seen a boy throw such a fit of temper."

"And the other times?"

"One time, it was a smell of burning. The third . . . Wait a minute . . . oh, yes . . . She had been listening at Monsieur's door and she hadn't heard his breathing. She sent me to make sure nothing had happened to him."

"Couldn't she have gone in herself?"

"I suppose she had her reasons. Mind you, I'm not complaining. Since she goes out in the afternoons and almost every evening, there are long periods of peace."

"Do you get on well with Lise?"

"Not too badly. She's a pretty girl. For a time . . . Well, you know what I mean . . . She needs to change . . . Almost every Saturday it's a different man. . . . Well, since I don't like to share . . ."

"What about Madame Vauquin?"

"That toad!"

"Doesn't she like you?"

"She measures out our food as if we were boarders, and she's even more miserly with the wine, no doubt because her husband's a drunk who beats her at least twice a week —naturally, she has it in for all men."

"Madame Marchand?"

"I hardly see her except when she's pushing her vacuum cleaner. That woman never talks, but she moves her lips whenever she's alone. Maybe she's praying."

"Mademoiselle?"

"She isn't proud or affected. It's a pity she's always so sad."

"Do you think she's having an unhappy love affair?"

"I don't know. Maybe it's just the atmosphere in the house. . . ."

"Have you heard about the letters?"

He seemed embarrassed.

"I may as well tell you the truth. . . . Yes. . . . But I haven't read them."

"Who told you about them?"

Even more embarrassed, he pretended to search his memory.

"I don't know. . . . I come, I go, I say a few words to someone, a few to someone else . . ."

"Was it Mademoiselle Vague?"

"No. She never talks about Monsieur's business."

"Monsieur Tortu?"

"That fellow thinks he's my boss all over again."

"Julien Baud?"

"Perhaps . . . Really, I don't remember. . . . It was maybe in the office . . ."

"Do you know whether there are any guns in the house?"

"Monsieur has a Browning in the drawer of his bedside table, but I haven't seen any cartridges in the room."

"Do you do his room?"

"That's part of my duties. I serve at table too, of course."

"Don't you know of any other gun?"

"There's Madame's little toy, a 6.33 made at Herstal. . . . You'd need to fire it point-blank to hurt anyone. . . ."

"Have you felt any change in the atmosphere in the house lately?"

He seemed to think.

"Possibly. They never talk much at the table. Now I might say they never talk at all. Only a few words between Monsieur Gus and Mademoiselle, from time to time . . ."

"Do you believe the letters?"

"About as much as I believe in astrology. According to the horoscopes in the paper, I ought to get a fat sum of money at least once a week. . . ."

"So you don't think that something might happen?"

"Not because of the letters."

"Because of what, then?"

"I don't know."

"Does Monsieur Parendon seem odd to you?"

"That depends on what you mean by odd. Everyone has his own idea about the life he leads. If he's happy that way . . . Anyway, he's not mad. I would even say, just the opposite. . . ."

"That she is the one who is mad?"

"Not that either. Good God! That woman is as wily as a fox."

"Thank you, Ferdinand."

"I do my best, Superintendent. I've learned that it pays to be honest with the police."

The door shut behind Maigret. He went down the broad staircase with its wrought-iron balustrade. He waved a hand to the concierge, who was braided like a hotel porter, and breathed the fresh air again with a sigh of relaxation.

He remembered a pleasant bar on the corner of the Avenue Marigny and the Rue du Cirque, and it wasn't long before he was leaning at the counter. He wondered what he would drink, and ended up by ordering a pint of beer. The atmosphere of the Parendons still stuck to him. But would it not have been the same if he had spent as much time with any family?

With less intensity, perhaps. He would doubtless have found the same spites, the same pettinesses, the same fears, in any case the same lack of cohesion.

"Don't philosophize, Maigret!"

Didn't he forbid himself to think, on principle? Good! He had not seen the two children, or the cook, or the cleaning-woman. He had only seen the maid in the distance, in a black uniform with a lace cap and apron.

Because he was on the corner of Rue du Cirque he remembered Dr. Martin, Parendon's personal physician.

"I suppose I should see him," he said to himself.

He caught sight of the name plate on the front of the building, climbed to the third floor, was shown into a waiting room where there were already three people, and, discouraged, came out again.

"Aren't you here to see the doctor?"

"I didn't come for a consultation. I'll telephone him."

"What name?"

"Superintendent Maigret."

"Wouldn't you like me to tell him that you are here?"

"I would rather not make his patients wait any longer than they have to. . . ."

There was the other Parendon, the brother, but he was a doctor too, and Maigret knew enough about the routine of Parisian doctors, through his friend Pardon.

He didn't want to take the bus or the métro. He felt weary, heavy with fatigue, and he let himself collapse into a taxi.

"Quai des Orfèvres. . . ."

"Yes, Monsieur Maigret. . . ."

That did not please him. He used to be rather proud of being recognized, but for some years he had been increasingly irritated by it.

What kind of fool would he look like if nothing happened in the house on the Avenue Marigny? He had not even dared to mention the letters at the briefing. For two days he had neglected his office and had spent most of his time in an apartment where the people led a kind of life that had nothing to do with him.

There were cases in progress, fortunately not very important ones, to which he should still be giving his attention.

Was it the letters, plus the midday telephone call, that were twisting his view of people? He could not think of Madame Parendon as an ordinary woman he might meet anywhere. He saw her again in his mind's eye, pathetic in all the blue of her boudoir and her housecoat, putting on some kind of act for his benefit.

Parendon, too, had stopped being an ordinary man. The gnome looked at him with his pale eyes made bigger by the thick lenses, and Maigret tried in vain to read his thoughts in them.

The others . . . Mademoiselle Vague . . . That big red-headed boy Julien Baud . . . Tortu looking suddenly at the door where Madame Parendon had appeared as if by magic.

He shrugged his shoulders and, since the car was coming to a stop in front of the main door of Police Headquarters, rummaged in his pockets for change.

*

Some ten inspectors filed into his office, each one with a problem to hand over to him. He opened the mail that had come in in his absence and signed a pile of documents, but all the time he was working in the sunny calm of his office the house on the Avenue Marigny remained in the back of his mind.

He felt an uneasiness that he could not throw off. And yet he had done everything he could. No crime, no misdemeanor had been committed. No one had called the police officially for a special reason. No one had lodged a complaint.

Nevertheless he had devoted hours to studying the little world that revolved around Emile Parendon.

He searched his memory in vain for a precedent. Yet he had dealt with all kinds of situations.

At a quarter past five someone brought him an express letter which had just arrived, and he recognized the block letters at once.

The stamp showed that the letter had been mailed at half past four at the post office on Rue de Miromesnil—that is to say, a quarter of an hour after he had left the Parendons' house.

He tore off the strip on the dotted line. Because of the size of the sheet, the writing was smaller than in the previous letters, and Maigret noted, comparing them, that this one had been written more quickly, less carefully, possibly in a feverish sort of haste.

"Dear Superintendent,

"When I wrote my first letter to you and asked you to give me your answer by means of an advertisement, I could not have imagined that you would charge headfirst into this case about which I had hoped later to give you indispensable details.

"Your haste has spoiled everything, and now you yourself must realize that you are all at sea. Today you have provoked the murderer in some way, and I am sure that he will feel obliged to strike because of you.

"I may be wrong, but I believe it will be sometime in the next few hours. I cannot help you. I am sorry. I do not hold it against you."

Maigret reread the letter with a grave expression on his face and went to the door to call Janvier and Lapointe. Lucas was not there.

"Read this, boys."

He watched them with some anxiety, as if to see if their reactions were the same as his. They had not been contaminated by the time spent in the apartment. They could only judge by the bits of evidence they had seen.

Leaning together over the sheet of paper, they showed an increasing interest and a growing alarm.

"It looks as if things are heating up," murmured Janvier, laying the express letter on the desk.

"What are these people like?" asked Lapointe.

"Like everybody else and like no one at all. . . . What I'm wondering is what we can do. I can't leave a man in the apartment permanently, and anyway that wouldn't do any good—the place is so vast that anything could happen in one part without someone in another part noticing. Have someone posted in the building? I'm going to do that tonight to ease my conscience, but, if the letters are not a joke, the blow won't come from outside. . . ."

"Are you free, Lapointe?"

"I haven't anything special on, Chief."

"Right, then you'll go. You'll find the concierge in the lodge, a man called Lamure who used to work on the Rue des Saussaies. Spend the night in his room and go up to the first floor from time to time. Get Lamure to give you a list of all the people living in the building, including the staff, and check all points of entry."

"I see."

"What do you see?"

"That this way, if anything happens, we'll at least have something to work on. . . ."

It was true, but the superintendent hated to look at the situation in that light. If anything happened . . . All right! Since it wasn't a question of theft, it could only be a death. . . . Whose death? Killed by whom?

People had talked to him, had answered his questions, had seemed to be telling the truth. Was it for him, dammit, to decide who was lying and who was telling the truth, or even if one of the people involved was crazy?

He strode up and down his office with furious steps and talked as if to himself, while Lapointe and Janvier exchanged glances.

"It's quite simple, Superintendent. . . . Someone writes to you and says that someone is going to kill. . . . The only thing is, he can't tell you in advance who will kill whom, or when, or how. . . . Why does he write to you?

Why warn you? For no reason at all. . . . To amuse himself. . . ."

He seized a pipe and filled it, tapping it nervously with
his index finger.

"Who does he take me for, anyway? If something happens, they'll say it's my fault. . . . That woman in blue
chiffon thinks it is already. . . . It seems I've gone to work
too quickly. . . . What should I have done?

"Waited for an invitation? All right! And if nothing
happens, *I* look like a fool, *I'm* the man who has wasted
the taxpayers' money for two days. . . ."

Janvier remained serious, but Lapointe could not help
smiling, and Maigret saw him. For a moment he stopped,
still angry, then he too laughed, slapping his assistant on
the shoulder.

"I'm sorry, boys. This case will drive me mad. Over
there everybody walks around on tiptoe and I began to
walk on tiptoe too, to tread as if I were walking on
eggs. . . ."

This time Janvier had to laugh too, imagining Maigret
walking on eggs.

"At least I can let off steam here. . . . That's it. . . .
Let's talk seriously. Lapointe, you can go now. Get something to eat and go and take up your post on Avenue Marigny. If anything at all odd happens, don't hesitate to telephone me at home, even if it should be the middle of the
night.

"Good night. See you tomorrow. Someone will relieve
you at about eight in the morning. . . ."

He went over to the window and stood there. With his

eyes following the course of the Seine, he went on for Janvier's benefit:

"Are you on any particular case at the moment?"

"I arrested the two boys this morning, two kids of sixteen. . . . You were right . . ."

"Will you take over from Lapointe tomorrow morning? It seems stupid, I know, and that's why I'm annoyed, but I feel obliged to take these precautions, which in any case don't serve any useful purpose.

"You'll see, if anything happens everyone will blame me. . . ."

While he spoke the last sentence he was staring at one of the lampposts on the Pont Saint-Michel.

"Give me the letter."

He had remembered a word, one he had not paid any attention to before, and he wondered if his memory was at fault.

"'. . . I am sure that he will feel obliged to strike because of you.'"

The word "strike" was indeed there. Obviously that could mean strike a hard blow. But, in the three letters, the anonymous correspondent had shown a certain meticulousness in his choice of words.

"Strike, you see? Both the man and the woman have a gun. I was in fact going to demand that they be handed over to us, the way I would take matches away from children. But I can't take away all their kitchen knives and all the paper knives. . . . One can strike with pokers too, and there is no lack of fireplaces there. . . . Or of candlesticks. . . . Or of statues. . . ."

Suddenly changing his tone, he said:

"Try to get me Germain Parendon on the phone. He's a neurologist on Rue d'Aguesseau, my Parendon's brother."

He lit his pipe while he waited. Janvier, sitting on a corner of the desk, fiddled with the telephone.

"Hello? Is this Dr. Parendon's house? . . . This is the Criminal Police, Mademoiselle. . . . Superintendent Maigret's office. . . . The superintendent would like to speak to the doctor for a moment. . . . What? . . . In Nice? . . . Yes. . . . Just a moment. . . ."

For Maigret was signaling to him.

"Ask her where he's staying."

"Are you still there? Could you tell me where the doctor is staying? . . . At the Négresco? . . . Thank you. . . . Yes, I expect so. . . . I'll try, anyway. . . ."

"Is he seeing a patient?"

"No. It's a conference on infantile neurology. It seems it's a very heavy program and the doctor has to give a paper tomorrow. . . ."

"Ring the Négresco. It's only six o'clock. . . . Today's program ought to be over. They're bound to have a big dinner somewhere at eight, at the Préfecture or somewhere else. If he isn't at a cocktail party . . ."

They had to wait ten minutes or so, because the Négresco's lines were always busy.

"Hello, this is Criminal Police, in Paris, Mademoiselle. . . . Could you get me Dr. Parendon, please. . . . Yes, Parendon. . . . He is one of the conference delegates. . . .

"She is going to see if he's in his room or at the cocktail

party which is going on just now in the main reception hall.

"Hello. . . . Yes, Doctor. . . . Excuse me, I'll hand you over to Superintendent Maigret."

Maigret took the receiver awkwardly, for at the last moment he didn't know what to say.

"I am sorry to disturb you, Doctor. . . ."

"I was just going to give my paper a last look-over. . . ."

"That's what I imagined you would be doing. I have spent a long time with your brother, yesterday and today. . . ."

"How did you two get together?"

The voice was gay, pleasant, much younger than Maigret had expected.

"It's quite complicated, and that's why I took the liberty of calling you. . . ."

"Is my brother in trouble?"

"Not as far as I know. . . ."

"Is he ill?"

"What is your opinion of his health?"

"He seems much weaker and frailer than he really is. I couldn't stand up under the amount of work he manages to get through in a few days. . . ."

Maigret decided to come to the point.

"I'll explain as briefly as I can what the situation is. Yesterday morning I received an anonymous letter telling me that a murder was going to be committed. . . ."

"At Emile's?"

The voice was full of laughter.

"No. It would take too long to tell you how we got to your brother's house. In any case, it turned out that that letter and the next did come from his house, both written on his writing paper, with the letterhead carefully cut off."

"I suppose my brother reassured you? It's a joke of Gus's, isn't it?"

"As far as I know, your nephew is not in the habit of playing practical jokes. . . ."

"That's true. Bambi isn't either. . . . I don't know . . . Maybe the young Swiss clerk? . . . Or a housemaid? . . ."

"I have just received a third message, an express letter this time. It says that the event is about to take place."

The doctor's tone changed.

"Do you believe it?"

"I've only known the household since yesterday. . . ."

"What does Emile have to say about it? I suppose he just shrugs it off?"

"He doesn't take it quite as lightly as that, really. On the contrary, I have the impression that he believes there's a real threat."

"Against whom?"

"Perhaps against himself. . . ."

"Who on earth would want to harm him? And why? Apart from his passion for the revision of Article 64, he's the most inoffensive, friendly soul in the world. . . ."

"I liked him very much. . . . You spoke of passion just now, Doctor. . . . Would you, as a neurologist, go so far as to say mania?"

"In the medical sense, certainly not."

His tone had become drier, for he had caught on to the superintendent's meaning.

"In fact, you are asking me if my brother is sane. . . ."

"I wouldn't have gone as far as that."

"Are you having the house guarded?"

"I have already sent one of my inspectors over."

"Has my brother had to deal with any shady characters lately? He hasn't set himself against business interests that are too powerful for him?"

"He didn't talk about his business affairs, but I know that this very afternoon he had a Greek shipowner and a Dutch one in his office."

"They come from as far away as Japan. . . . We can only hope it is just a joke. . . . Have you any other questions to ask me?"

Maigret had to think quickly, as the neurologist at the other end of the line was probably looking at the Promenade des Anglais and the blue waters of the Baie des Anges.

"What is your opinion of your sister-in-law's stability?"

"Between ourselves, and I would certainly not repeat it in the witness box, if all women were like her, I would have remained a bachelor. . . ."

"I said her stability. . . ."

"I understood that. Let's say that she goes to extremes in everything . . . and, to be fair, I must admit that she is the first to suffer for it. . . ."

"Is she the kind of woman to have fixed opinions?"

"Certainly, if those opinions are plausible and spring from precise facts. I can assure you that if she told you a lie, it was so perfect a lie that you haven't noticed it. . . ."

"Would you say she is a hysteric?"

There was a fairly long silence.

"I wouldn't quite dare to go so far, although I've seen her in states which could be called hysterical. Mind you, although she is neurotic, she manages by some kind of miracle to find the strength to control herself."

"Did you know she has a gun in her room?"

"She told me about it one evening. She even showed it to me. It's more of a toy than anything else."

"A deadly toy. Would you let her keep it in her drawer?"

"You know, if she took it into her head to kill, she would manage it in any case, with or without a firearm."

"Your brother has a gun, too."

"I know."

"Would you say the same thing about him?"

"No. I am sure, not just as a man, but as a doctor, that my brother would never kill. . . . The only thing that might happen would be that he might kill himself one evening in a fit of despair. . . ."

His voice had cracked.

"You're very fond of him, aren't you?"

"There are just the two of us. . . ."

The sentence struck Maigret. Their father was still alive, and Germain Parendon too was married. Now he said:

"There are just the two of us. . . ."

As if each one had only the other in the world. Was the brother's marriage also a wretched one?

Parendon, in Nice, pulled himself together. Perhaps he had looked at his watch.

"Well! Let's hope nothing happens. Good-by, Monsieur Maigret."

"Good-by, Dr. Parendon."

The superintendent had telephoned to reassure himself. But what had happened had just the opposite effect. He felt more worried than ever after his talk with the lawyer's brother.

"The only thing that might happen . . . one evening in a fit of despair . . ."

And was it precisely that which was going to happen?

What if it were Parendon himself who had written the anonymous letters? To stop himself from acting? To put a kind of barrier between the impulse and the act?

Maigret had forgotten Janvier, who had taken up his stand near the window.

"Did you hear that?"

"I heard what you said. . . ."

"He doesn't like his sister-in-law. He believes that his brother would never kill anyone, but he is less sure that he wouldn't be tempted to commit suicide some day. . . ."

The sun had set, and it was suddenly as if something was missing. It was not yet dark. There was no need to put on the lights. The superintendent did so anyway, as if to chase the evil spirits away.

"Tomorrow you will see the house and you'll understand better. There's nothing to stop you from phoning and telling Ferdinand who you are and walking around the apartment and in the offices. . . . They are prepared for it. . . . They expect it. . . .

"The only thing that might happen would be that Madame Parendon might appear in front of you when you least expected it—I almost believe she gets around without even displacing air. . . . Well, she'll look at you and you will feel vaguely guilty. That's the impression she makes on everybody."

Maigret called the office boy to give him the signed documents and the letters to post.

"Nothing new? No one to see me?"

"No one, Superintendent."

Maigret was not expecting any visitors. But he was surprised that neither Gus nor his sister had appeared at any time. They, like the rest of the household, must be fully aware of what had happened since the previous day. They would certainly have heard people talking about Maigret's questionings. Perhaps they had even seen him rounding a corner in the hall?

If Maigret, at fifteen, had heard someone say . . .

He would of course have hastened to question the superintendent thoroughly, ready to take over from him.

He realized that time had passed, that that was in another world.

"Shall we have a drink at the Brasserie Dauphine and go home for dinner?"

That is what they did. Maigret walked a good bit of the way before taking a taxi, and when his wife, on hearing his footsteps, opened the door, he did not look particularly oppressed.

"What is there to eat?"

"Lunch warmed up."

"And what was there for lunch?"

"Cassoulet."

They both smiled, but she had guessed his state of mind nevertheless.

"Don't worry, Maigret. . . ."

He hadn't told her anything more about the case he was working on. Aren't all cases the same, when you get right down to it?

"You're not the one who's responsible. . . ."

After a moment, she added:

"It gets cold suddenly at this time of year. . . . I'd better close the window. . . ."

5

As on every other morning, his first contact with life was the smell of coffee, then his wife's hand touching his shoulder, and finally the sight of Madame Maigret, already fresh and alert, wearing a flowered housecoat, holding his cup out to him.

He blinked and asked, rather stupidly:

"The telephone hasn't rung, has it?"

If it had, he would have come awake as quickly as she. The curtains were drawn back. Spring, though it had come early, was still there. The sun was up and the noises of the street stood out clearly.

He gave a sigh of relief. Lapointe had not telephoned. Therefore nothing had happened on Avenue Marigny. He drank half the cup, got up briskly, and went into the bathroom. He had been wrong to worry. When the first letter arrived, he should have realized that it was not serious.

This morning he was a little ashamed of having let himself panic like a child who still believes in ghost stories.

"Did you sleep well?"

"Very well."

"Do you think you'll be back for lunch?"

"I think so."

"Would you like fish?"

"Skate in black butter, if you can get any."

Half an hour later, when he pushed open the door of his office, he was surprised and annoyed to find Lapointe in the armchair. The poor boy was a bit pale and almost asleep. He had chosen to wait rather than leave a report and go home to bed, no doubt because the superintendent had seemed so worried the night before.

"Well, Lapointe, my boy?"

The inspector had got up when Maigret sat down in front of the pile of letters on his desk.

"Just a minute, please . . ."

He wanted to reassure himself first of all that there was no new anonymous letter.

"Good! Now tell me . . ."

"I got there a little before six in the evening and made contact with Lamure, the concierge, who insisted that I have dinner with him and his wife. The first person to come into the building after me, at ten past six, was young Parendon, the one they call Gus."

Lapointe pulled a notebook out of his pocket so that he could refer to his notes.

"Was he alone?"

"Yes. He had several schoolbooks under his arm. Then, a few minutes later, an effeminate-looking man carrying a leather bag . . . Lamure told me that it was the Peruvian woman's hairdresser.

" 'There must be a ball or a big party somewhere,' he said calmly, and drained his glass of red wine.

"By the way, he emptied a bottle by himself and he was surprised, and a bit annoyed, that I didn't do the same.

"Let's see. . . . At seven forty-five a woman arrived in a chauffeur-driven car—Madame Hortense, the concierge called her.

"She's one of Madame Parendon's sisters, the one she goes out with most often. She's married to a Monsieur Benoît-Biguet, an important man, very rich, and they have a Spanish chauffeur. . . ."

Lapointe smiled.

"I'm sorry to be giving you these uninteresting details, but since I had nothing else to do I wrote everything down. . . . At eight thirty the Peruvians' limousine drew up and the couple came down in the elevator. He was wearing tails and she wore a formal evening gown with a chinchilla stole. You don't see that sort of thing very often now. . . .

"At five to nine Madame Parendon and Madame Hortense went out. I found out afterward where they went— the chauffeurs are in the habit of coming in for a drink at the lodge with Lamure when they get back. He always has a liter of red wine at hand. . . .

"There was a charity bridge evening at the Crillon Hotel, and that's where they went. They came back shortly after midnight. The sister went upstairs and stayed there for half an hour. That's when the chauffeur came in for his drink.

"Nobody paid any attention to me. I just looked like one of them, no one of importance. . . . The hardest thing was not to empty the glasses I was given.

"Mademoiselle Parendon—they call her Bambi—came in at about one o'clock. . . ."

"When did she go out?"

"I don't know. I didn't see her leave. That means she didn't have dinner at home. She was accompanied by a young man whom she kissed at the foot of the stairs. . . . She wasn't at all embarrassed by our being there. . . .

"I asked Lamure if she always did that. He said she did, and it was always the same boy, but he didn't know who he was. . . . He was wearing a leather jacket and shapeless moccasins, and his hair was on the long side. . . ."

Lapointe sounded as if he was repeating by rote, fighting sleep, his eyes on his notebook.

"You haven't mentioned the departure of Mademoiselle Vague, Tortu, and Julien Baud. . . ."

"I didn't write it down, really, because I thought it was part of the routine. They came down at six o'clock, by the stairs, and once on the sidewalk they each went their own way."

"What else?"

"I went up as far as the fourth floor two or three times, but I saw and heard nothing. I could have been wandering about in a church at night.

"The Peruvians came in at about three o'clock. They'd

115

had supper at Maxim's. Before that they had been to a big movie opening on the Champs-Elysées. It seems they're real in-people.

"That's all that happened at night. Not even a cat, one really can say that, because there isn't an animal in the place except for the Peruvians' parakeet.

"Did I tell you that Ferdinand, the Parendons' butler, went off to bed at about ten, and that the cook left at nine o'clock?

"It was Ferdinand who appeared first in the morning, at seven o'clock. He went out, because he usually goes to the bar at the corner of Rue du Cirque to have his first coffee of the day, and fresh croissants. . . . He was gone for about half an hour. During that time the cook arrived, and the cleaning-woman, Madame Marchand.

"The chauffeur came over from his room, which is over the garage, near Ferdinand's, and went upstairs for breakfast. . . .

"I didn't write everything down right away. That's why my notes are a bit confused. During the night I went to listen at the Parendons' door at least ten times, and I didn't hear a thing.

"The Peruvians' chauffeur brought out his employers' car to wash it, just as he does every morning. . . ."

Lapointe put his notebook back in his pocket.

"That's all, Chief. Janvier came. I introduced him to Lamure, who seemed to know him already, and I left. . . ."

"Well, get to bed quickly now. . . ."

In a few moments the bell for the briefing would ring in

the corridors. Maigret filled a pipe, grabbed his paper knife, and went swiftly through the mail.

He was relieved. He had every reason to be. But there was still a sinking feeling in the pit of his stomach, a vague apprehension.

The main subject under discussion in the director's office was the son of a Minister of State who had had a car crash at four in the morning, at the corner of Rue Fran-çois Ier, in unpleasant circumstances. Not only was he drunk, but the name of the girl with him, who had had to be taken to a hospital, could hardly be revealed without causing a scandal. As for the driver of the car that had been run into, he had died instantly.

"What's your opinion, Maigret?"

"Me? Nothing, sir."

When it was a matter of politics or of anything concerning politics, Maigret just played possum. He had the knack of looking vague, almost stupid, at such times.

"Still, we must find an answer. . . . The newspapers don't know anything about it yet, but in an hour or two they will. . . ."

It was ten o'clock. The telephone on the director's desk rang. He picked it up nervously.

"Yes, he's here. . . ."

He held the receiver out to Maigret:

"It's for you. . . ."

He had a premonition. He knew before putting the receiver to his ear that something had happened on Avenue Marigny, and it was indeed Janvier's voice at the other end of the line. It was low, almost as if he were embarrassed.

"Is that you, Chief?"

"Yes, it's me. . . . Well, who is it?"

Janvier understood the meaning of his question at once.

"The young secretary. . . ."

"Dead?"

"Unfortunately."

"Shot?"

"No. . . . There was no noise. . . . No one noticed anything. . . . The doctor hasn't got here yet. . . . I'm calling you before I have any details because I was downstairs when it happened. . . . Monsieur Parendon is here beside me; he's quite shattered. . . . We're waiting for Dr. Martin to arrive at any moment."

"Was she stabbed?"

"More like butchered. . . ."

"I'll be right over."

The director and Maigret's colleagues looked at him, surprised to see him so pale, so affected by the call. At the Quai des Orfèvres, particularly in the Criminal Division, didn't they deal in murder daily?

"Who is it?" asked the director.

"Parendon's secretary."

"The neurologist?"

"No. His brother, the lawyer. . . . I'd had some anonymous letters."

He pushed through the door without giving any more explanations and went straight to the inspectors' office.

"Lucas?"

"Yes, Chief . . ."

He looked around.

"You, Torrence . . . Right. . . . You two come into my office. . . ."

Lucas, who knew about the letters, asked:

"Has there been a murder?"

"Yes."

"Parendon?"

"His secretary. . . . Ring Moers and tell him to get over there with his technicians. . . . I'm calling the Public Prosecutor's Office. . . ."

It was always the same. For at least an hour, instead of working in peace, he was going to have to give explanations to the deputy public prosecutor and to whichever examining magistrate was appointed.

"Carry on, fellows. . . ."

He was overcome, as if it had been someone in his own family. Of all the members of the household, Mademoiselle Vague was the last he would have thought of as the victim.

He had taken a liking to her. He liked the way she had spoken of her relationship with her employer, a mixture of jauntiness and matter-of-factness. He had sensed that at bottom, in spite of the difference in ages, she felt for him a passionate loyalty which is perhaps one of the truest kinds of love.

Then why was she the one to be killed?

He climbed into the little black car while Lucas took the wheel and big Torrence got in behind.

"What's it all about?" he asked as they moved off.

"You'll find out," replied Lucas, who knew how Maigret was feeling.

Maigret didn't notice the streets, the passers-by, the trees which were growing greener every day, the huge buses which passed dangerously close to their car.

He was there already. He visualized Mademoiselle Vague's little office, where he had sat by the window at the same time on the previous day. She had sat right opposite him, as if to show him the sincerity in her eyes. And when she had hesitated after a question it was because she was searching for the right words.

There was a car at the door already. It belonged to the local superintendent, whom Janvier must have notified. For, whatever happens, the correct procedure must be followed.

Lamure was standing gloomily in the doorway of his luxurious lodge.

"Who would have thought . . . ?" he began.

Maigret walked past him without answering and started up the stairs, since the elevator was at one of the other floors. Janvier was waiting for him on the landing. He said nothing. He too could guess how his chief was feeling. Maigret didn't notice Ferdinand, at his post as if nothing had happened, taking his hat.

He strode into the hall, passed the door of Parendon's office, and came to Mademoiselle Vague's, which was standing open. At first he saw only two men, the local superintendent, Lambilliote, whom he had met frequently, and one of his colleagues.

He had to look at the floor, almost under the Louis XIII table which was used as a desk.

She was wearing an almond-green spring frock, probably for the first time that season, since on the previous day and the day before that he had seen her in a navy-blue skirt and a white blouse. He had thought that she must consider it a kind of uniform.

After the blow she must have slid out of her chair, and her body was doubled over, oddly twisted. Her throat was gaping open and she had lost a considerable quantity of blood, which would still be warm.

It took him some time to realize that Lambilliote was shaking his hand.

"Did you know her?"

He looked at Maigret, astounded to see him so moved by the sight of a body.

"Yes, I knew her," he said in a hoarse voice.

And he rushed into the office at the end of the corridor where Julien Baud, eyes reddened, stood before him. His breath smelled of spirits. There was a bottle of brandy on the desk. In the corner René Tortu held his head in his hands.

"Was it you who found her?"

The word *"tu"* came naturally to his lips, since the big Swiss seemed suddenly like a child.

"Yes, sir."

"Did you hear anything? Did she cry out? Did she groan?"

"Nothing . . ."

He could hardly speak. There was a lump in his throat and tears poured from his blue eyes.

"Excuse me. . . . It's the first time . . ."

It seemed as though he had been waiting to cry until that moment, and he pulled his handkerchief from his pocket.

"I . . . Just a minute. . . . I'm sorry. . . ."

He wept copiously, standing in the middle of the room, looking taller than his five foot eleven. There was a sharp little sound. It was the stem of Maigret's pipe breaking under the pressure of his bite. The bowl fell to the floor. He bent down to pick it up and put it in his pocket.

"Please forgive me. . . . I couldn't help it. . . ."

Baud got his voice back, dried his eyes, and glanced at the bottle of brandy but didn't dare touch it.

"She came in here at about ten past nine to bring me some documents to check. Incidentally, I can't remember where I put them. It's the proceedings of yesterday's session, with notes and references. . . . I must have left them in her office. . . . No. . . . Oh! They're on my table. . . ."

Creased by a clenched hand.

"She asked me to take them back to her as soon as I had finished. I went in. . . ."

"At what time?"

"I don't know. . . . I must have worked for about half an hour. . . . I was very happy, very pleased with life. . . . I like working for her. . . . I looked around. . . . I didn't see her. . . . Then, when I looked down . . ."

Maigret poured a little brandy into the glass which Ferdinand must have brought and gave it to him.

"Was she still breathing?"

He shook his head.

"The men from the Public Prosecutor's Office are here, Chief."

"Didn't you hear anything either, Monsieur Tortu?"

"No, nothing . . ."

"Were you in here all the time?"

"No. . . . I went to see Monsieur Parendon for about ten minutes about the case I dealt with at the Law Courts yesterday. . . ."

"What time was that?"

"I didn't look at my watch. . . . About nine thirty . . ."

"How was he?"

"The same as usual. . . ."

"Was he alone?"

"Mademoiselle Vague was with him. . . ."

"Did she go out as soon as you came in?"

"A few seconds later. . . ."

Maigret would have liked a brandy too, but he didn't dare ask for one.

He had to go through the formalities. He grumbled about it, but in fact it wasn't a bad thing because it made him come out of the nightmare he was living in.

The Public Prosecutor's Office had appointed Daumas as examining magistrate. Maigret had worked with him several times, a pleasant man, a little on the timid side, whose only fault was excessive attention to detail. He must have been about forty. With him was the deputy public prosecutor, De Claes, a tall, fair man, very thin, perfectly turned out. He always held a pair of light-colored gloves in his hand, summer and winter.

"What do you think, Maigret? I'm told you had an inspector in the building, is that right? Were you expecting anything to happen?"

Maigret shrugged his shoulders and gestured vaguely.

"It would take too long to tell you everything. . . . I spent almost all day in this apartment yesterday and the day before, following up some anonymous letters."

"Did the letters say who the victim would be?"

"No, that's just it. That's why it was impossible to avoid the murder. I would have had to have a policeman standing behind each person, following them step by step through the house. Lapointe spent the night downstairs. This morning Janvier took his place. . . ."

Janvier was standing in a corner, his head bowed. From the courtyard came the sound of the Peruvians' chauffeur washing the Rolls.

"Who did tell you, Janvier?"

"Ferdinand. He knew I was down there. . . . I had spoken to him. . . ."

There were heavy footsteps in the hall. The experts had arrived with their apparatus. One little man, completely spherical, didn't seem to fit in with the group, and he looked at all the people in the room, wondering which one to speak to.

"Dr. Martin," he murmured finally. "I'm sorry to have got here so late, but I had a patient in my office and she took so long to get dressed . . ."

He saw the body. He opened his bag and knelt on the floor. He was the least moved of anyone.

"She's dead, of course."

"Did she die instantly?"

"She must have lived for a few seconds, let's say thirty or forty seconds, and since her throat was cut she couldn't possibly have cried out."

He pointed to an object half hidden by the table. It was the scraping knife Maigret had noticed the previous day. Now it was stuck in the pool of thick blood.

In spite of himself, the superintendent looked at the girl's face, her glasses askew, her eyes blue and staring.

"Would you close her eyes, Dr. Martin?"

Except at the beginning of his career, he had rarely been so shaken by the sight of a corpse.

As the doctor was about to obey, Moers plucked at Maigret's sleeve.

"The photographs," he reminded him.

"Of course . . . No, don't do anything. . . ."

It was up to him not to look. They still had to wait for the medical expert. Dr. Martin, a lively man in spite of his stoutness, asked:

"May I go now, gentlemen?"

Then, looking at each in turn, he finally addressed Maigret.

"Are you Superintendent Maigret? I wonder if I shouldn't go and see Monsieur Parendon. Do you know where he is?"

"In his office, I imagine."

"Does he know? . . . Has he seen? . . ."

"Probably."

In fact, no one knew anything for certain. The whole atmosphere was one of incoherence. A photographer set up an enormous camera on a tripod while a gray-haired man took measurements on the floor and the magistrate's clerk scribbled in a notebook.

Lucas and Torrence, who had not yet received any instructions, stood in the hallway.

"What do you think I should do?"

"Go and see him if you think he might need you."

Dr. Martin had just reached the door when Maigret called him back.

"I will undoubtedly have questions to ask you sometime today. Will you be at home?"

"Except between eleven and three—I have a clinic at the hospital."

He pulled out a fat pocket watch, looked startled, and went off rapidly.

Judge Daumas coughed.

"I suppose, Maigret, you'd rather I left you to work in peace? I only wanted to know if you suspect anyone in particular. . . ."

"No. . . . Yes. . . . Frankly, sir, I don't know. This case isn't like any other I have had, and I'm a little confused. . . ."

"Do you need me any more?" asked Superintendent Lambilliote.

"Not any more," Maigret replied vaguely.

He was in a hurry to see them all go. The office emptied

little by little. Suddenly a flashbulb went off in the already bright room. Two men, going about their work as matter-of-factly as carpenters or locksmiths, took fingerprints of the dead girl.

Maigret slipped quietly out of the room, signaled to Lucas and Torrence to wait for him, and went into the office at the end of the hall, where Tortu was answering the telephone while Baud, his elbows on the table, stared blankly in front of him.

He was drunk. The level of the brandy in the bottle had gone down by three good fingers. Maigret picked it up and, quite unashamedly, because it was really necessary, poured himself a drink in the Swiss boy's glass.

He went about his work like a sleepwalker, stopping at times, his eyes staring blankly, afraid that he might have forgotten something essential. He shook hands absent-mindedly with the medical expert, whose real work would begin only at the Medico-Legal Institute.

The ambulance men were already there with a stretcher, and Maigret took a last glance at the almond-green dress that had been meant to celebrate a lovely spring day.

"Janvier, you'd better see to her parents. Their address must be there, in the office at the end of the hall. Look in her handbag, too. . . . Anyway, do what has to be done. . . ."

He led the other two men toward the cloakroom.

"You two draw me up a plan of the apartment, then question everyone in it and note down where each person

was between nine fifteen and ten. And take down everything everybody saw, everyone who went out and
in. . . ."

Ferdinand was standing there waiting, his arms folded.

"He will help you with the plan. Tell me, Ferdinand, I
suppose Madame Parendon is in her room?"

"Yes, Monsieur Maigret."

"How did she react?"

"She didn't react at all, sir, because she doesn't know
anything about it yet. As far as I know she is sleeping, and
Lise hasn't dared take it on herself to waken her."

"Hasn't Monsieur Parendon gone to see her either?"

"Monsieur hasn't left his office."

"Hasn't he seen the body?"

"Excuse me. He did leave it for a minute, when Monsieur Tortu went to tell him. He took a quick look into
Mademoiselle Vague's office and then went back to his
own."

Maigret had been wrong the previous evening in believing that because his anonymous correspondent had a
precise style he should take the word "strike" literally.

She hadn't been struck. Nor had she been shot. She had
literally been slaughtered.

He had to move aside to let the stretcher-bearers pass,
and a few moments later he knocked at the enormous door
of Parendon's office. He heard no reply. Still, it was a thick
oak door. He turned the knob, pushed on one of the pan-
els, and saw the lawyer sitting in one of the leather armchairs.

For a second he was afraid that something terrible had

happened to him too, he was so bent over, his chin resting on his chest, one soft hand touching the carpet.

Maigret walked over and sat in a chair opposite him so that they were face to face, close together, just as they had been at their first meeting. On the shelves, the gilt-lettered names of Lagache, Henri Ey, Ruyssen, and other psychiatrists shone brightly on the leather bindings.

He was surprised to hear a voice murmur:

"What do you think about it, Monsieur Maigret?"

The voice was remote, dull. It was the voice of a man prostrated with grief. The lawyer could scarcely make the effort to sit up or to raise his head. Suddenly his glasses fell to the ground, and without the thick lenses his eyes looked like those of a frightened child. He bent forward to pick them up with an effort and put them on again.

He spoke again:

"What are they doing?"

And he pointed with his white hand to the girl's office.

"The formalities are over. . . ."

"The . . . the body?"

"They have just taken the body away."

"Don't worry. . . . I'm going to pull myself together."

He placed his right hand automatically over his heart while the superintendent looked at him as fixedly as he had on the first day.

Parendon managed to pull himself together, took a handkerchief out of his pocket, mopped his face with it.

"Would you like something to drink?"

He looked toward the part of the paneling that hid a little bar.

"Will you have one too?"

Maigret took advantage of the offer to get up and take out two glasses and the bottle of armagnac.

"It wasn't a joke," the lawyer said slowly.

Although his voice had grown strong again, it was still strange, mechanical, without any ring.

"It puts you in an awkward position, doesn't it?"

And, since Maigret still stared at him without answering, he added:

"What are you going to do now?"

"Two of my men are busy establishing how everyone in the apartment spent the time between nine fifteen and ten o'clock. . . ."

"It happened before ten o'clock. . . ."

"I know."

"Ten to ten. . . . It was exactly ten to ten when Tortu came in and told me. . . ."

He glanced at the bronze clock, which showed twenty-five minutes to twelve.

"Did you stay in that chair after that?"

"I followed Tortu down the hall, but I couldn't stand the sight for more than a few seconds. . . . I came back here and . . . You are right. . . . I haven't moved from this chair. . . .

"I vaguely remember that Dr. Martin came in, that he spoke to me, that I shook my head, that he took my pulse and left in a hurry. . . ."

"He had to go to the hospital for his clinic, as a matter of fact."

"He must have thought that I was drugged."

"Have you ever taken anything like that?"

"Never. I can imagine what it's like."

The trees outside rustled softly, and one could hear the rumble of the buses on the Place Beauveau.

"I could never have suspected . . ."

He spoke incoherently, leaving his sentences unfinished, and Maigret kept on staring at him. Maigret always carried two pipes in his pocket, and he took out the unbroken one, filled it, and puffed deeply, as if to recover his equilibrium.

"Suspected what?"

"How far . . . In what way . . . The importance . . . Yes, the importance, that's the word, of relationships. . . ."

His hand pointed once more to the secretary's office.

"It was so unexpected!"

Would Maigret have been any surer of himself if he had read all the books on psychiatry and psychology on the library shelves?

He could not remember ever having watched a man as intensely as he did at that moment. He did not miss a movement, not a twitch of a facial muscle.

"Did you think it would be she?"

"No," admitted the superintendent.

"Did you think it would be me?"

"You or your wife."

"Where is *she*?"

"Apparently she is asleep and doesn't yet know anything about it."

The lawyer frowned. He was making a great effort to concentrate.

"Hasn't she left her rooms?"

"Not according to Ferdinand."

"It isn't part of Ferdinand's duties . . ."

"I know. One of my inspectors is probably questioning Lise right now."

Parendon began to grow agitated, as if something he had not previously thought of had suddenly worried him.

"Well then, are you going to arrest me? If my wife didn't leave her room . . ."

Had it then seemed evident to him that Madame Parendon was the murderer?

"Tell me, are you going to arrest me?"

"It is too soon to arrest anyone."

He got up and swallowed a mouthful of armagnac, wiping the back of his hand across his forehead.

"I don't understand anything any more, Maigret. . . ."

He took a grip on himself.

"Excuse me . . . Monsieur Maigret . . . Did anyone who doesn't belong to the household get into the apartment?"

He was returning to his normal self again. His eyes were growing lively.

"No. One of my men spent the night in the lodge, and another relieved him at about eight this morning."

"We must read the letters again," Parendon murmured.

"I read them several times late yesterday afternoon."

"There is something that doesn't hang together in all this, as if events suddenly took an unexpected turn. . . ."

132

He sat down again, and Maigret considered what he had said. He too, when he learned that Mademoiselle Vague was dead, had thought that it was a mistake.

"You know, she was very, very . . . devoted to me."

"More than that," affirmed the superintendent.

"Do you think so?"

"When she spoke to me of you yesterday, she spoke with real passion."

The little man blinked, incredulous, as if he could not believe that he had inspired such feelings.

"I had a long talk with her while you were seeing the two shipowners."

"I know. She told me. . . . What had happened to the documents?"

"Julien Baud had them in his hand when he discovered the body and rushed back to his office in a panic. The papers are a bit crumpled."

"They are very important. Those people must not suffer because of what has happened in my house."

"May I ask you a question, Monsieur Parendon?"

"I have been waiting for it ever since I saw you come in. It is your duty to ask it, of course, and also not to take my word for it. . . . No, I did not kill Mademoiselle Vague.

"There are words that I have hardly ever spoken in my life, which I have almost erased from my vocabulary. Today I am going to use one, because there is no other to express the truth which I have just discovered. I loved her, Monsieur Maigret."

He said that calmly, and it was all the more impressive. The rest was more easily said.

"I thought I felt no more than a slight attachment for her, apart from physical desire. I was a little ashamed of it, because I have a daughter who is almost as old as she was. Antoinette had . . ."

That was the first time Maigret had heard anyone say Mademoiselle Vague's Christian name.

"She had a kind of . . . wait a minute . . . of spontaneity that I found refreshing. . . . You see, there is hardly any spontaneity in this house. She brought it in from outside, like a present, as one might bring in fresh flowers."

"Do you know with what weapon the crime was committed?"

"A kitchen knife, I suppose?"

"No. . . . A type of scraping knife that I noticed on your secretary's desk yesterday. . . . It caught my eye because it isn't the usual model. The blade is longer, sharper. . . ."

"It comes from the Papeterie Roman, like all the office supplies."

"Did you buy it?"

"Certainly not. She must have chosen it herself."

"Mademoiselle Vague was sitting at her desk, probably going over some documents. She had given some to Julien Baud to check."

Parendon did not seem like a man on his guard, a man expecting to be trapped. He listened carefully, possibly rather surprised at the importance Maigret attached to these details.

"The person who killed her knew that the scraping

knife was there in the pen-tray, or he would have brought a gun. . . ."

"What makes you think that he wasn't armed and then changed his mind?"

"Mademoiselle Vague saw him pick up the knife, and that did not make her suspicious. She did not get up. She went on working while he walked behind her. . . ."

Parendon was thinking, reconstructing in his mind the scene that Maigret had just described, with the precision of the great business lawyer that he was.

There was nothing woolly in his attitude. A gnome he might be, if one can poke fun at people of small stature, but a gnome of astonishing intelligence.

"I think you'll be obliged to arrest me before the day is over," he said suddenly.

There was nothing sarcastic in his manner. He had come to a certain conclusion after weighing up the pros and cons.

"It will be a chance for my counsel," he added, with some irony this time, "to get some practice on Article 64."

Maigret was confused once more. He was even more so when the door leading to the big drawing room opened and Madame Parendon stood in the doorway. She had not done her hair or put on any make-up. She wore the same blue housecoat as the day before. She was holding herself very erect, but she still looked much older than she was.

"I am sorry to disturb you. . . ."

She spoke as if nothing had happened.

"I suppose, Superintendent, that I have no right to

speak to my husband alone? We do not often do so, but under the circumstances . . ."

"For the moment I can only allow you to speak to him in my presence."

She did not come forward into the room but remained standing, the sun-filled drawing room behind her. The two men had got up when she appeared.

"Very well. You are doing your job."

She took a puff at the cigarette she was holding and looked hesitatingly at each in turn.

"May I first ask you, Monsieur Maigret, if you have come to a decision?"

"On what?"

"On what happened this morning. . . . I have just heard about it and I suppose you are about to make an arrest. . . ."

"I have not made any decision."

"Good. The children will be home soon, and it would be better to have everything clear. Tell me, Emile, was it you who killed her?"

Maigret could not believe his eyes or his ears. They were facing each other, ten feet apart, their expressions hard, their features strained.

"Are you daring to ask me if . . . ?"

Parendon choked, his little fists clenched with rage.

"Stop play-acting. Answer me yes or no."

Then, suddenly, he lost his temper, a thing that had probably happened to him very few times in his life, and, raising his arms in a sort of entreaty to heaven, he shouted:

"You know very well I did not, for God's sake!"

He was dancing with rage. He was almost on the point of attacking her.

"That is all I wanted to hear. Thank you."

And she went back into the drawing room in a most natural manner, closing the door behind her.

6

"I am sorry I lost my temper, Monsieur Maigret. It is most unusual for me. . . ."

"I know."

It was precisely because he knew it that Maigret was thoughtful.

The little man, still standing, got back his breath and his self-control and wiped his face once more. It was not flushed, but yellowish.

"Do you hate her?"

"I don't hate anybody. . . . Because I don't believe that a human being is ever fully responsible. . . ."

"Article 64!"

"Yes, Article 64 . . . I don't care if it makes me appear to be mad, but I will not change my opinion. . . ."

"Even if it should concern your wife?"

"Even if it should concern her."

"Even if she killed Mademoiselle Vague?"

138

For a moment his face seemed to dissolve, his eyes to dilate.

"Even then."

"Do you think she is capable of such an action?"

"I am not going to accuse anyone."

"A few moments ago I asked you a question. I am going to ask you another, and you will be able to answer yes or no. My anonymous correspondent is not necessarily the murderer. Someone, sensing disaster, might have thought that by introducing the police into the house he could avert it."

"I can anticipate the question. I did not write the letters."

"Could the murdered girl have done so?"

He reflected for a few moments.

"It's not impossible. But it doesn't fit in with her character. She was more direct than that—I was just telling you about her spontaneity. . . .

"In fact, wouldn't she have been more likely to come to me, since she knew quite well . . . ?"

He bit his lip.

"Knew what quite well?"

"That if I had felt I was being threatened I would have done nothing about it."

"Why?"

He looked hesitantly at Maigret.

"It's hard to explain. . . . One day I made my choice. . . ."

"By getting married?"

"By embarking on my chosen career. . . . By getting

married. . . . By living in a certain way. . . . So I must take the consequences. . . ."

"Isn't that contrary to your views on human responsibility?"

"Perhaps. It would seem so, anyway. . . ."

He seemed tired, helpless. One could guess at the turmoil of thoughts he was forcing himself to organize behind his domed forehead.

"Do you believe, Monsieur Parendon, that the person who wrote to me thought that the victim would be your secretary?"

"No."

In spite of the closed doors they heard a voice in the drawing room, crying:

"Where is my father?"

Then almost immediately the door opened abruptly and a very tall young man with unkempt hair took two or three steps into the room and stopped in front of the two men.

He first looked from one to the other, then his eyes became fixed on the superintendent with an almost menacing gleam.

"Are you going to arrest my father?"

"Calm down, Gus. . . . Superintendent Maigret and I . . ."

"Are you Maigret?"

He looked at him with more than mere curiosity.

"Whom are you going to arrest?"

"No one, at the moment."

"Anyway, I can swear it wasn't my father. . . ."

"Who told you what has happened?"

"The concierge first of all, but he didn't give me any details, then Ferdinand. . . ."

"Weren't you half expecting it?"

Parendon took advantage of the situation to sit down at his desk, as if he wanted to be in his most accustomed place once more.

"Is this an interrogation?"

And the boy turned to his father to ask his advice.

"My role, Gus . . ."

"Who told you I'm called Gus?"

"Everybody I've met here. . . . I'm going to ask you questions, just as I shall do with everybody, but it isn't an official interrogation. . . . I asked you if you weren't half expecting it?"

"Expecting what?"

"What happened this morning."

"If you mean was I expecting someone to cut Antoinette's throat, no. . . ."

"Did you call her Antoinette?"

"I've called her that for a long time. We were good friends."

"What did you expect?"

His ears suddenly flamed.

"Nothing in particular. . . ."

"But something drastic?"

"I don't know. . . ."

Maigret noted that Parendon was watching his son carefully, as if he too had asked a question, or as if he was making a discovery.

141

"Are you fifteen, Gus?"

"I'll be sixteen in June."

"Would you rather I talked to you in front of your father, or alone in your room or any other room?"

The boy hesitated. Although his anger had subsided, he was still very nervous. He turned toward the lawyer again.

"Which would you prefer, Father?"

"I think you would both be more at ease in your room. . . . Just a minute, Gus. . . . Your sister will be coming in at any minute, if she isn't here already. . . . I want you to have lunch together as usual, without worrying about me. . . . I won't come to the dining room."

"Aren't you going to have anything to eat?"

"I don't know. I may have a sandwich. . . . I need a little peace."

The boy was on the point of rushing to give his father a hug. It was not Maigret's presence that stopped him, but a fear, which must always have stood between father and son, of showing too much emotion.

Neither of them was inclined to sentimental effusions or embraces, and Maigret could easily visualize a younger Gus coming to sit silent and motionless in his father's office, just to watch him reading or working.

"If you want to come to my room, come on. . . ."

As they went through the drawing room, Maigret found Lucas and Torrence waiting for him, ill at ease in the enormous, sumptuously furnished room.

"Finished, fellows?"

"Yes, Chief. . . . Do you want to see the layout and the time schedule?"

"Not just now. What time did it happen?"

"Between half past nine and quarter to ten. . . . Almost certainly at nine thirty-seven."

Maigret turned toward the wide-open windows.

"Were they open this morning?" he asked.

"From a quarter past eight onward."

Behind the garages rose the many windows of a six-story apartment house on the Rue du Cirque. It was the back of the building. A woman was walking across a kitchen, pot in hand. Another, on the third floor, was changing her baby's diaper.

"You two go and have a bite before going on with the work. Where is Janvier?"

"He has found the mother, in a village in Berry. She hasn't got a telephone, and he has asked someone to get her to the post office. . . . He's waiting in the rear office for the call."

"He can join you later. You'll find a pretty good restaurant on Rue de Miromesnil—it's called 'Au Petit Chaudron.' After you've eaten, divide the floors of the apartment house you can see from here on the Rue du Cirque between you. Question the tenants whose windows look out on this side. They might, for instance, have seen someone going through the drawing room between nine thirty and nine forty-five. . . . They must be able to look into other rooms. . . ."

"Where will we find you?"

"At the Quai, when you've finished. Unless you find something important. . . . I might still be here."

Gus waited, interested in what was going on. The tragedy that had taken place did not stop him from having a slightly childish curiosity about police procedure.

"Now I'm all yours, Gus."

They went down a hallway, narrower than the one in the other wing, past a kitchen. They could see a fat woman dressed in black through the glass-paneled door.

"It's the second door."

The room was big, its whole feeling different from the rest of the apartment. The furniture was in the same style, undoubtedly because it had had to be used somewhere. Gus had changed its character by piling it up with all kinds of things, adding pinboards and shelves.

There were four loud-speakers, two or three phonograph turntables, a microscope on a white wood table, copper wires forming a complicated circuit fixed onto another table. There was only one armchair, by the window, with a piece of red cotton thrown haphazardly over it. There was a length of red cotton covering the bed, too, turning it into a sort of couch.

"You've kept it?" Maigret remarked, pointing to a large teddy bear on a shelf.

"Why should I be ashamed of it? My father gave it to me for my first birthday."

He spoke the word "father" proudly, almost defiantly. He was ready to spring fiercely to his defense.

"Did you like Mademoiselle Vague, Gus?"

"I've told you already. She was my friend."

He must have been flattered that a girl of twenty-five should treat him as a friend.

"Did you often go into her office?"

"At least once a day."

"Did you ever go out with her?"

The boy looked at him, surprised. Maigret filled his pipe.

"Go out where?"

"To the movies, maybe . . . or dancing . . ."

"I don't dance. I've never been out with her."

"Did you ever go to her apartment?"

The boy's ears flamed again.

"What are you trying to make me say? What are you thinking?"

"Did you know of Antoinette's relationship with your father?"

"Why not?" he replied, his head held proudly. "Do you see anything wrong with that?"

"It doesn't matter what I think, but what you think."

"My father's a free agent, isn't he?"

"What about your mother?"

"It wasn't any of her business."

"What do you mean by that?"

"It's a man's right . . ."

He didn't finish the sentence, but what he had said showed his meaning clearly.

"Do you think that's the reason for what happened this morning?"

"I don't know."

"Were you expecting something to happen?"

Maigret had taken a seat in the red chair, and he lit his pipe slowly, watching the boy, who was still in the adolescent period of growth, his arms too long, his hands too big.

"I was expecting it and not expecting it. . . ."

"Express yourself more clearly. Your teachers at the Lycée Racine would not accept that for an answer."

"I didn't imagine you were like this. . . ."

"Do you think I'm hard?"

"I think you don't like me, that you suspect me of something, I don't know what. . . ."

"That's right."

"Not of having killed Antoinette, though? Besides, I was at school."

"I know. And I also know that you really worship your father."

"Is that wrong?"

"Not at all. At the same time, you feel he's defenseless."

"What are you insinuating?"

"Nothing bad, Gus. Your father is inclined not to fight, except possibly in his work. He believes that everything that happens to him happens only because of his own shortcomings."

"He's an intelligent and honest man. . . ."

"Antoinette was defenseless too, in her own way. In fact there were two of you keeping guard over your father, she and you. That's why there was a sort of complicity between you."

"We never said anything about that. . . ."

"I'm sure you didn't. But you still felt you were on the same side. That's why, even if you had nothing to say to her, you never missed a chance of going to see her."

"What are you getting at?"

For the first time the boy, who had been fiddling with a piece of copper wire, did not meet his eyes.

"I'm there already. It was you who sent me those letters, Gus, and you who telephoned the Criminal Police yesterday."

Maigret could only see his back. There was a long pause. Finally the boy turned to him, his face scarlet.

"Yes, it was me. . . . You would have found out anyway, wouldn't you?"

He no longer looked defiantly at Maigret. On the contrary, the superintendent had risen in his esteem again.

"How did you come to suspect me?"

"The letters could only have been written by the murderer or by someone who was trying to protect your father indirectly."

"It could have been Antoinette."

Maigret thought it better not to tell him that the girl wasn't a child any more and would not have gone about things in such a complicated, or such a childish, way.

"Have I been a disappointment to you, Gus?"

"I thought you would go about things differently."

"How, for instance?"

"I don't know. I've read all about your cases. I thought you were the man who would understand everything. . . ."

"And now?"

"Now I don't think anything at all."

"Whom did you want me to arrest?"

"I didn't want you to arrest anyone."

"Well, then? What should I have done?"

"You're the one who's in charge of the Crime Squad, not me."

"Had any crime been committed yesterday, or even at nine o'clock this morning?"

"Of course not."

"What did you want me to protect your father from?"

There was another silence.

"I felt he was in danger."

"What kind of danger?"

Maigret was sure that Gus understood the real meaning of the question. The boy had wanted to protect his father. From whom? Couldn't it also have been to protect him from himself?

"I don't want to answer any more questions."

"Why not?"

"Because!"

He added, in a firm voice:

"Take me to the Quai des Orfèvres if you want. Ask me the same questions for hours on end. . . . Maybe you think I'm only a boy, but I swear I won't say any more. . . ."

"I'm not asking you any more. It's time you were going to lunch, Gus."

"It won't matter if I'm late back to school today."

"Where is your sister's room?"

"Two doors along this hallway."

"No hard feelings?"

"You're doing your job. . . ."

And the boy slammed the door. A moment later Maigret knocked at Bambi's door, through which he could hear the droning of a vacuum cleaner. It was a young girl in uniform who opened the door. She had soft blonde hair.

"Were you looking for me?"

"Are you Lise?"

"Yes. I'm the maid. You've already walked past me in the halls."

"Where is Mademoiselle Bambi?"

"She might be in the dining room. Or perhaps in her father's room, or her mother's—that's in the other wing."

"I know. I was in Madame Parendon's rooms yesterday."

An open door showed him a dining room paneled from floor to ceiling. The table, which could have seated twenty, was set for two. In a little while Bambi and her brother would be here, separated by a vast stretch of tablecloth, with Ferdinand, formal in white gloves, to serve them.

As he passed, he opened the door of the lawyer's office slightly. Parendon was sitting in the same chair as in the morning. There was a bottle of wine, a glass, and some sandwiches on a folding table. He did not move. Perhaps he had not heard anything. There was a spot of sunlight on his head. It looked bald like that.

The superintendent shut the door again and found the corridor he had gone along the day before, and the door of the boudoir. Through it he could hear a voice he did not recognize, insistent, tragic.

He could not make out the words, but he could feel the unbridled passion.

He knocked very loudly. The voice stopped suddenly and a second later the door opened and a girl stood in front of him, still breathless, her eyes shining.

"What do you want?"

"I am Superintendent Maigret."

"I thought so. So what? Haven't we the right to be in our own house any more?"

She was not beautiful, but she had a pleasant face and a well-proportioned figure. She wore a simply cut suit, and her hair was held back by a ribbon, although it was not the fashion.

"I would like to have a short talk with you before you have lunch, Mademoiselle."

"Here?"

He hesitated. He had seen her mother's shoulders trembling.

"Not necessarily. Wherever you like."

Bambi came out of the room without a backward glance, shut the door, and said:

"Where do you want to go?"

"To your room?" he suggested.

"Lise is doing my room."

"To one of the offices?"

"I don't mind."

Her hostility was not directed toward Maigret in particular. It was more a state of mind. Now that her violent harangue had been interrupted, her nerves had relaxed and she followed him dully.

"Not in . . ." she began.

Not in Mademoiselle Vague's room, of course. They

went into Tortu's and Julien Baud's office. They were out having lunch.

"Have you seen your father? Sit down."

"I'd rather not sit."

She was too overwrought to sit still in a chair.

"As you like."

He did not sit either, but leaned on Tortu's desk.

"I asked you if you had seen your father?"

"No, not since I came home."

"When did you get back?"

"At twelve fifteen."

"Who told you what had happened?"

"The concierge."

It appeared that Lamure had lain in wait for both Gus and his sister, so as to be the first to tell them the news.

"And then?"

"And then what?"

"What did you do?"

"Ferdinand wanted to say something to me. I didn't listen and I went straight to my room."

"Was Lise there?"

"Yes. She was cleaning the bathroom. Everything's late because of what has happened."

"Did you cry?"

"No."

"Didn't it occur to you to go and see your father?"

"Maybe. . . . I don't remember. . . . I didn't go."

"Did you stay in your room long?"

"I didn't look at the time. Five minutes, maybe a little longer. . . ."

"What were you doing?"

She looked at him, hesitating. That seemed to be a habit in the household. Everyone had a tendency to weigh his words before he spoke.

"Looking in the mirror."

It was a challenge. That habit, too, could be found in other members of the family.

"Why?"

"You want me to be honest, don't you? Well, I will be. . . . I was trying to see whom I look like."

"You mean your father or your mother?"

"Yes."

"What conclusion did you come to?"

Her expression hardened and she shouted at him angrily:

"My mother!"

"Do you hate your mother, Mademoiselle Parendon?"

"I don't hate her. I want to help her. I've often tried."

"To help her do what?"

"Do you think this is getting us anywhere?"

"What are you talking about?"

"Your questions . . . My answers . . ."

"They may help me to understand."

"You spend a few hours here and there in the midst of a family and you think you can understand them? Don't think I'm hostile to you. I know you have been wandering around the house since Monday."

"Do you know who sent me the letters?"

"Yes."

"How did you find out?"

"I walked in while he was cutting the sheets of paper."

"Did Gus tell you what they were for?"

"No. I only understood afterward, when I heard people talking about the letters."

"Who told you about them?"

"I don't remember. Julien Baud, maybe. I like him. He looks scatterbrained, but he's a nice boy."

"There's one thing that intrigues me. . . . It was you who chose the nickname Bambi and who called your brother Gus, wasn't it?"

She looked at him, smiling slightly.

"Does that surprise you?"

"Was it a protest?"

"That's right. A protest against this huge, solemn barracks of a place, against the way we live, against the kind of people who come here. . . . I wish I'd been born in an ordinary family and had to struggle to make my way in life."

"You are struggling, in your own way."

"Archaeology, as you know. I didn't want to take up a career where I would be taking a place from someone else."

"It's your mother who irritates you above all, isn't it?"

"I would much rather not talk about her."

"Unfortunately, she is what matters just now, isn't she?"

"Perhaps. . . . I don't know. . . ."

She stole a glance at him.

"You think she is guilty," Maigret insisted.

"What makes you think that?"

"When I went to her room I heard you speaking angrily. . . ."

"That doesn't mean that I think she's guilty. . . . I don't like the way she behaves. . . . I don't like the life she leads, the life she makes us lead. . . . I don't like . . ."

She was less in control of herself than her brother, although she looked calmer.

"Do you blame her for not making your father happy?"

"You can't make people happy in spite of themselves. As for making them unhappy . . ."

"Did you like Mademoiselle Vague, as you like Julien Baud?"

She didn't hesitate before replying.

"No!"

"Why?"

"Because she was a little schemer who made my father believe she loved him."

"Did you ever hear them speak of love?"

"Certainly not. She wouldn't coo over him in front of me. You only had to see her when she was with him. I don't know what went on when the door was closed."

"Were you upset on moral grounds?"

"To hell with morals. . . . And anyway, what morals? . . . Those of what environment? Do you think that the moral standards of this district are the same as those of a small town in the provinces or those of the 20th *Arrondissement?*"

"Do you think she hurt your father?"

"Perhaps she isolated him too much."

"Do you mean that she estranged him from you?"

154

"Those are questions I've never thought about. Nobody thinks about them. Let's say that if she hadn't been there, there might have been some chance . . ."

"Of what? Of a reconciliation?"

"There wasn't anything to reconcile. My parents have never loved each other, and I don't believe in love either. Nevertheless there is a possibility of living in peace, in a kind of harmony. . . ."

"Is that what you have tried to bring about?"

"I've tried to calm my mother's frenzies, to lessen her rantings and ravings. . . ."

"Hasn't your father helped you?"

Her ideas were not at all like those of her brother, and yet they coincided on a few points.

"My father has given up."

"Because of his secretary?"

"I'd rather not answer that, not say any more. Put yourself in my place—I come home from the Sorbonne and I find . . ."

"You're right. Believe me, I am doing this so that the least possible harm will come of it. Can you imagine an investigation dragging on for several weeks, the uncertainty, the interviews at Criminal Police, then in the magistrate's office . . ."

"I hadn't thought of that. What are you going to do?"

"I haven't made any decisions yet."

"Have you had lunch?"

"No. Neither have you, and your brother must be waiting for you in the dining room."

"Isn't my father having lunch with us?"

"He'd rather have it alone in his office."

"Aren't you having lunch?"

"I'm not hungry just now, but I must confess I'm dying of thirst."

"What would you like to drink? Beer? Wine?"

"Anything, as long as it's in a big glass. . . ."

She couldn't help smiling.

"Wait here a minute. . . ."

He had understood the reason for her smile. She didn't see him going to the kitchen or the butler's pantry to have a drink, like one of the servants. Nor did she see him sitting with Gus and herself in the dining room while they lunched in silence.

When she came back, he saw she hadn't bothered with a tray. She held a bottle of Saint-Emilion, six years old, in one hand, and a cut-glass tumbler in the other.

"Don't hold it against me if I was rude to you, or if I haven't been very helpful. . . ."

"You are all very helpful. . . . Run along and eat now, Mademoiselle Bambi."

It was an odd sensation to be there at one end of the apartment, in the office belonging to Tortu and the young Swiss, alone with a bottle and a glass. Because he had said a big glass, she had brought a water tumbler and he was not ashamed of filling it full.

He was really thirsty. He needed some kind of stimulation too, for he had just spent one of the most exhausting mornings of his career. Now he was sure that Madame Parendon was waiting for him. She knew that he had questioned the entire household except for her, and she would be waiting restlessly, wondering when he would finally come.

Had she, like her husband, had lunch taken to her room?

He sipped his wine standing in front of the window, looking vaguely at the courtyard, which he saw for the first time empty of cars, with only a ginger cat stretched out in a patch of sunlight. Since Lamure had told him that except for the parakeet there wasn't an animal in the house, it must be a neighbor's cat, looking for a peaceful spot.

He hesitated before taking a second glass, filled it half full, and took time to fill a pipe before drinking it.

After that he heaved a sigh and went to the boudoir, along the hallways he was now familiar with.

He had no need to knock. His steps had been heard in spite of the carpet, and the door opened as soon as he approached. Madame Parendon, still wearing her blue silk housecoat, had had time to put on her make-up and do her hair, and her face looked almost as it had the previous day.

Was it more tense or more relaxed? He would have found it difficult to say. He felt there was a difference, some sort of flaw, but he was unable to pick it out.

"I was expecting you."

"I know. Well, now I am here. . . ."

"Why did you have to see everyone else before me?"

"What if it was to give you time to think things over?"

"I don't need to think things over. . . . To think what things over?"

"The things that have happened. . . . The things that are inevitably going to happen. . . ."

157

"What are you talking about?"

"When a murder has been committed it is followed, sooner or later, by an arrest, a preliminary investigation, a trial. . . ."

"What has that got to do with me?"

"You hated Antoinette, didn't you?"

"So you call her by her Christian name too?"

"Who else does?"

"Gus, for one. I don't know about my husband. . . . He's probably capable of saying 'Mademoiselle' very politely while making love."

"She's dead."

"Well? Just because someone is dead do we have to see nothing but good in her?"

"What did you do last night when your sister left after bringing you back from the Crillon?"

She frowned, remembered, sneered:

"I had forgotten that you had filled the house with policemen. . . . Well . . . I had a headache, I took an aspirin and tried to read while I waited for it to take effect. See, the book is still there, and you'll find a bookmark at page ten or twelve. . . . I didn't get very far. . . .

"I went to bed and tried to sleep, without success. . . . That happens not infrequently and my doctor knows all about it."

"Dr. Martin?"

"Dr. Martin is my husband's doctor, and the children's. My doctor is Dr. Pommeroy, who lives on Boulevard Haussmann. I'm not ill, thank God!"

She spoke these words forcefully, threw them out like a challenge.

"I'm not undergoing any treatment or following any diet. . . ."

He thought she was going to say, under her breath:

"Unlike my husband."

She did not say it, and went on:

"The only thing I have to complain about is insomnia. Sometimes I am still awake at three in the morning. . . . It's both tiring and a strain. . . ."

"Was that the case last night?"

"Yes. . . ."

"Were you worried?"

"By your visit?" she retorted in a flash.

"It might have been by the anonymous letters, by the atmosphere they had created. . . ."

"I have slept badly for years, and there were never any anonymous letters. . . . I always end up by getting up again and taking a sleeping pill that Dr. Pommeroy has prescribed for me. If you want to see the box . . ."

"Why should I want to see it?"

"I don't know. Judging by the questions you asked me yesterday, I can expect anything. . . . In spite of the sleeping pill, it took me a good half hour to get to sleep, and when I woke up I was surprised to see that it was half past eleven."

"I thought you often got up late."

"Not as late as that. I rang for Lise. . . . She brought me a tray with tea and toast. It wasn't until she opened the curtains that I saw her eyes were all red.

"I asked her why she had been crying. She burst into tears again and told me that something dreadful had happened, and I at once thought of my husband. . . ."

"What did you think might have happened to him?"

"Do you think that man is strong? Don't you think that his heart might give out at any moment, like the rest?"

He did not comment on "like the rest," but reserved it for later.

"She finally told me that Mademoiselle Vague had been murdered and that the house was full of policemen."

"What was your first reaction?"

"I was so shattered that I began by drinking my tea. Then I rushed to my husband's office. What's going to happen to him?"

He pretended not to understand.

"To whom?"

"To my husband. You aren't going to throw him in prison? With his health . . ."

"Why should I put your husband in prison? In the first place, that's not my job, but the judge's. Furthermore, I don't see any reason at this moment for arresting your husband."

"Well, whom do you suspect, then?"

He did not answer. He walked slowly over the blue carpet with its yellow pattern while she sat down, as she had done the day before, in the easy chair.

"Why, Madame Parendon," he asked, putting emphasis on each syllable, "would your husband have killed his secretary?"

"Must there have been a reason?"

"One doesn't usually commit murder without a motive."

"Some people could imagine a motive, couldn't they?"

"Such as . . . ?"

"For example, if she were pregnant?"

"Do you have any reason to believe that she was pregnant?"

"None. . . ."

"Is your husband a Catholic?"

"No. . . ."

"Even suppose she had been pregnant, it's quite possible that he might have been very pleased. . . ."

"It would have been an embarrassment to him."

"You forget that we no longer live in the times when unmarried mothers were looked down on. Times change, Madame Parendon. . . . Then, too, many people have no hesitation in finding a broad-minded gynecologist. . . ."

"I only used that as an example."

"Think of another reason."

"She might have been blackmailing him. . . ."

"For what reason? Are your husband's business affairs shady? Do you believe he is capable of serious irregularities which might cast a slur on his honor as a member of the Bar?"

She resigned herself, tight-lipped, to saying:

"Certainly not."

She lit a cigarette.

"That kind of girl always ends up trying to make the man marry her."

"Has your husband spoken to you about a divorce?"

"Not so far."

"What would you do if he did?"

"I would feel obliged to resign myself to it and to stop taking care of him. . . ."

"I understand you have considerable means of your own. . . ."

"More than he does. This is my house. I own the whole building."

"In that case I can see no reason for blackmail."

"Perhaps he was growing tired of a make-believe love?"

"Why make-believe?"

"Because of his age, his background, his kind of life, everything. . . ."

"Is your love more real?"

"I gave him two children."

"Do you mean you gave them to him as a wedding present?"

"Are you daring to insult me?"

She looked furiously at him again while he, on the other hand, took care to appear calmer than he was.

"I have no such intention, Madame, but it usually takes two people to make children. Let us say more simply that you and your husband have had two children."

"What are you trying to get at?"

"I am trying to get you to tell me simply and sincerely what you did this morning."

"I have told you."

"Neither simply nor sincerely. You told me a long story about insomnia, so that you could skip over the whole morning."

"I was asleep."

"I would like to be sure about that. . . . I will probably know for certain in a very short time. My inspectors have taken note of what everyone did, and where, between nine fifteen and ten. I am well aware that one can get to the offices by different routes."

"Are you accusing me of lying?"

"Of not telling me the whole truth, at least."

"Do you think my husband is innocent?"

"I don't think anyone is innocent, *a priori,* just as I don't think anyone is guilty. . . ."

"Yet the way you are interrogating me . . ."

"What was your daughter accusing you of when I came to look for her?"

"Didn't she tell you?"

"I didn't ask her."

She sneered once more. It was a bitter twist of the lips, an ironical smile that she wanted to be cruel, scornful.

"She is luckier than I am."

"I asked you what she was accusing you of. . . ."

"Of not being beside her father at a time like this, if you must know."

"Does she think that her father is guilty?"

"What if she does?"

"Gus too, of course?"

"Gus is still at the age where the father is a kind of god and the mother is a shrew."

"When you appeared in your husband's study just now, you knew I would be there with him. . . ."

"You aren't necessarily everywhere, Monsieur Maigret,

and I might have wanted to see my husband alone. . . ."

"You asked him a question. . . ."

"A simple question, a natural question, the question any wife in my position would have asked in the same circumstances. You saw his reaction, didn't you? Did you think it was normal? Would you say that a man who dances with rage, shouting insults, is a normal man?"

She felt that she had scored a point and she lit another cigarette after stubbing out the first in a blue marble ashtray.

"I am waiting for your other questions, if you have any more to ask. . . ."

"Have you had lunch?"

"Don't worry about that. If you are hungry . . ."

Her expression, as well as her attitude, was capable of changing from one moment to the next. She became very much the woman of the world again. Leaning back slightly, her eyes half closed, she was mentally snapping her fingers at him.

7

Maigret had managed to keep himself under control from the beginning of his interview with Madame Parendon. And it was sadness that overcame his irritation little by little. He felt clumsy, awkward. He realized how much he lacked knowledge of the world which might have helped him carry out this interrogation more smoothly.

Finally he sat down in one of the chairs that were too delicate for him, his unlit pipe in his hand, and said in a calm but lifeless voice:

"Listen to me, Madame. Contrary to what you may think, I am not your enemy. I am only a civil servant whose job is to look for the truth with the means at his disposal.

"I am going to ask you again the question I asked you a moment ago. I must ask you to think before you answer, to weigh the pros and cons. I must warn you that if it is later proved that you have lied to me, I shall draw my own conclusions and I shall ask the judge for a warrant for your arrest."

He watched her, particularly her hands, which betrayed her inner tension.

"Did you leave your rooms after nine o'clock this morning, and did you go in the direction of the offices, for any reason whatsoever?"

She did not blink, did not turn her eyes away. She took her time, as he had asked, but it was obvious that she was not thinking, that she had already taken her stand once and for all. Finally she said:

"No."

"You did not set foot in the halls?"

"No."

"You did not go through the drawing room?"

"No."

"You did not, even with no evil intent, go into Mademoiselle Vague's office?"

"No. I may add that I consider these questions an insult."

"It is my duty to ask them."

"You forget that my father is still alive. . . ."

"Is that a threat?"

"I am simply reminding you that you are not in your office at the Quai des Orfèvres. . . ."

"Would you rather I took you there?"

"I dare you to. . . ."

He thought it better not to take her at her word. He often went fishing when he was at Meung-sur-Loire, and once he had landed an eel which he had tremendous difficulty in taking off the hook. It kept slipping between his fingers, and finally it fell on the grass on the bank and slid back into the water.

He was not here for his own pleasure. He was not fishing.

"Do you then deny having killed Mademoiselle Vague?"

The same words, over and over, the same look of a man who is desperately trying to understand another human being.

"You know perfectly well."

"What do I know?"

"That it was my poor husband who killed her."

"For what reason?"

"I have already told you. . . . In his condition, there is no need for a precise reason. . . .

"I am going to tell you something which I alone know, apart from him, because he told me before we were married. He was afraid of the marriage. He put it off time and time again. At that time I didn't know that he was consulting several doctors.

"Did you know that when he was seventeen he tried to commit suicide because he was afraid he wasn't a normal man? He cut his wrist. When the blood spurted out he panicked and called for help, pretending there had been an accident. . . .

"Do you know what this tendency to suicide means?"

Maigret was sorry that he had not brought the bottle of wine with him. Tortu and young Julien Baud must have been surprised to find it in their room when they came back, and they would probably have emptied it by now.

"He had scruples. . . . He was afraid that our children wouldn't be normal. When Bambi began to grow, and to talk, he watched her anxiously. . . ."

It might have been true. There was certainly some truth in what she was saying, but he still had the impression of a sort of displacement, of a split between the words, the sentences, and the truth.

"He is haunted by the fear of illness and death. Dr. Martin knows about that. . . ."

"I saw Dr. Martin this morning."

She appeared to register the blow, then quickly regained her assurance.

"Didn't he mention it to you?"

"No. And he did not for one moment think that your husband could be the murderer."

"You are forgetting a doctor's professional secrets, Superintendent."

He began to see a glimmer of light, but she remained vague, distant.

"I also spoke to his brother on the telephone. He is in Nice, at a conference."

"Was that after what has happened?"

"Before."

"Wasn't he concerned?"

"He did not advise me to have your husband watched."

"And yet he must know . . ."

She lit yet another cigarette. She was chain-smoking, inhaling deeply.

"Have you never met people who have lost contact with

life, with reality, who turn in on themselves rather as one turns a glove inside out?

"Question our friends, both men and women. Ask them if my husband takes any interest now in human beings. He does dine with some people, because I insist, but he hardly notices that they are there, and as for speaking to them . . .

"He doesn't listen, he sits as if he were shut in. . . ."

"Are the friends you are speaking of the friends of his choice?"

"They are people whom we, in our position, ought to meet, normal people who lead a normal life. . . ."

He did not ask her what she considered a normal life. He felt it better to let her go on talking. Her monologue was growing more and more interesting.

"Do you think that he went to the beach even once last summer, or to the swimming pool? He spent his time sitting under a tree in the garden. What I took for distraction, when I was a girl, when he suddenly stopped listening to me, is a real inability to live with other people.

"That is why he shuts himself in his office, why he hardly comes out of it, and when he does he looks at us like an owl surprised by the light.

"You have been quick to judge, Monsieur Maigret. . . ."

"I have another question to ask you. . . ."

He was sure before he asked it what the answer would be.

"Have you handled your revolver since yesterday evening?"

"Why should I have handled it?"

"I am waiting for an answer from you, not a question."

"The answer is no."

"How long is it since you held it in your hand?"

"Months. . . . It's a long time since I tidied up that drawer."

"You handled it yesterday, when you showed it to me."

"I had forgotten that."

"But, since I handled it, my fingerprints will be on top of the others."

"Is that all you have found out?"

She looked at him as if she were disappointed at discovering that Maigret was so stupid, so bad at his job.

"You have just told me, with a certain self-satisfaction, of your husband's isolation and of his lack of contact with reality. Now, as recently as yesterday he was in his office dealing with an extremely important case with men who most certainly have their feet on the ground. . . ."

"Why do you think he chose Maritime Law? He has never set foot on a boat in his life. . . . He has no contact with seamen. . . . Everything takes place on paper. Everything is abstract, don't you see? It's another proof of what I keep telling you, of what you refuse to see. . . ."

She got up and began to pace about the room as if she were thinking.

"Even his hobby, the celebrated Article 64—isn't that proof that he is afraid, afraid of himself, and that he is trying to reassure himself? He knows that you are here, that you are questioning me. . . . In this house everyone is aware of what everyone else is doing. . . . Do you know what he is thinking? . . . He is hoping that I will become impatient, that I will appear nervous, that I will get angry, so that I will be suspected instead of him. . . .

"If I were in prison, he would be free. . . ."

"Just a minute. I don't understand. What freedom would he have that he doesn't have now?"

"His complete freedom."

"To do what, now that Mademoiselle Vague is dead?"

"There are other Mademoiselle Vagues."

"So now you think that your husband would take advantage of your being away from home to have mistresses?"

"Why not? It's another way of reassuring oneself. . . ."

"By killing them one after the other?"

"He wouldn't necessarily kill the others."

"I thought you said he was incapable of making contact with people."

"With normal people, people of our social standing. . . ."

"So people who are not of your social standing are not normal?"

"You know very well what I mean. I mean that it is not normal for him to seek their company."

"Why not?"

Someone knocked at the door. It opened to reveal Ferdinand in a white jacket.

"One of the gentlemen wishes to speak to you, Monsieur Maigret."

"Where is he?"

"Here, in the hall. He told me it was extremely urgent, and so I took the liberty of bringing him. . . ."

The superintendent could make out Lucas's figure in the darkened passage.

"Will you excuse me, Madame Parendon?"

He shut the door behind him while Ferdinand disappeared and the lawyer's wife remained alone in her room.

"What is it, Lucas?"

"She went through the drawing room twice this morning."

"Are you sure?"

"You can't see it from here, but from the drawing room you can, quite clearly. . . . There is an invalid who sits almost all day at one of the windows on Rue du Cirque. . . ."

"A very old man?"

"No. It's a man who had an accident to his legs. He's about fifty. He is interested in everything that goes on in this house, and the car washing, especially when it's the Rolls, fascinates him. Judging by his replies to the other questions I asked him, we can believe what he says. . . . His name is Montagné. . . . His daughter is a midwife. . . ."

"At what time did he see her first?"

"Shortly after nine thirty."

"Was she going toward the offices?"

"Yes. He is more familiar than we are with the layout of the place. That's how he knows about Parendon and his secretary. . . ."

"What was she wearing?"

"A blue housecoat."

"And the second time?"

"She went through the room in the opposite direction less than five minutes later. One detail struck him—the maid was dusting at the far end of the room and she didn't see her. . . ."

"Madame Parendon didn't see the maid?"

"No."

"Have you questioned Lise?"

"Yes, this morning."

"Didn't she mention the incident?"

"She says she didn't see anything."

"Thank you. . . ."

"What shall I do now?"

"You can both wait here for me. Was there any confirmation of what the man Montagné said?"

"Only a young maid on the fifth floor who thinks she saw something blue at the same time."

Maigret knocked on the boudoir door and went in just as Madame Parendon was coming out of her bedroom. He took time to empty his pipe and fill it again.

"Would you be so good as to ring for your maid?"

"Do you need something?"

"Yes."

"As you wish."

She pressed a button. Several minutes passed in silence, and Maigret, watching the woman he was tormenting, could not help having a constricted feeling in his chest.

He went over in his mind the terms of Article 64, which had taken on such importance in the past three days:

"If the person charged with the commission of a felony or misdemeanor was then insane or acted by absolute necessity, no offense has been committed."

Could the man Madame Parendon had just described to him, her husband, have acted in a state of dementia at any given moment?

Had she too read the books on psychiatry, or . . . ?

Lise came in, visibly afraid.

"Did you send for me, Madame?"

"The superintendent wishes to speak to you."

"Shut the door, Lise. There's nothing to be afraid of. . . . When you answered my inspectors' questions this morning you were upset, and you obviously did not realize how important their questions were."

The poor girl looked from the superintendent to her mistress, who was sitting in the easy chair, her legs crossed, leaning back, as if it had nothing to do with her.

"I don't know what you are talking about. . . ."

"The actions of all the staff between nine fifteen and ten o'clock have been established. Shortly after nine thirty, let's say at nine thirty-five, you were dusting in the drawing room. Is that right?"

Another look at Madame Parendon, who did not look at her, then a faint voice:

"Yes, it's true."

"At what time did you go into the drawing room?"

"About nine thirty. . . . A little later. . . ."

174

"So you didn't see Madame Parendon going in the direction of the offices?"

"No."

"But shortly after you got there, when you were at the far end of the room, you saw her going in the opposite direction, that is to say, going toward these rooms. . . ."

"What should I do, Madame?"

"That is your affair, my child. Answer the questions put to you. . . ."

Tears were flowing down Lise's cheeks. She had rolled the handkerchief she had taken from her apron pocket into a ball.

"Did someone tell you something?" she asked naïvely.

"Answer the question, as Madame has just advised you. . . ."

"Will it mean that Madame is charged?"

"It will confirm another witness's statement, someone who lives on Rue du Cirque and who saw both of you from his window."

"Oh, well, there's no point in lying. It's true. I'm sorry, Madame. . . ."

She wanted to rush to her mistress, possibly to throw herself on her knees, but Madame Parendon spoke coldly to her.

"If the superintendent has finished with you, you may go."

She went out and burst into tears in the doorway.

"What does that prove?" asked the woman, on her feet again, a cigarette trembling at her lips, her hands in the pockets of her blue housecoat.

"That you have lied at least once."

"I am in my own house and I do not have to give an account of my actions."

"In a case of murder, you do. I warned you when I asked you the question."

"Does that mean you are going to arrest me?"

"I am going to ask you to come with me to the Quai des Orfèvres."

"Have you a warrant?"

"A blank one. A summons where I have only to write in your name."

"And then?"

"That won't depend on me any more."

"On whom?"

"On the magistrate. Then, probably, on the doctors."

"Do you think I am mad?"

He read the panic in her eyes.

"It isn't up to me to answer that."

"I am not mad, do you hear? . . . And even if I did kill her, which I still deny, it was not in a moment of madness. . . ."

"May I ask you to give me your revolver?"

"Get it yourself. It's in the top drawer of my dressing table."

He went into the bedroom. Everything there was pale pink. The two rooms, one blue, the other pink, reminded him of a painting by Marie Laurencin.

The bed, a big low bed, Louis XVI in style, was still unmade. The furniture was painted a pale gray. On the dressing table he saw pots of cream, little bottles, the whole range of products women use to fight the ravages of time.

He shrugged his shoulders. This intimate display made him melancholy. He thought of Gus, who had written the first letter.

Would things have happened in the same way if he had not intervened?

He took the revolver out of the drawer, in which there were also jewel-boxes.

He did not know how to answer the question. Would Madame Parendon perhaps have attacked her husband instead of attacking the girl? Would she have waited a few days more? Would she have used another weapon?

He frowned as he went back into the boudoir where the woman was standing in front of the window, her back to him. He saw that her back was beginning to bend. Her shoulders seemed narrower, bonier.

He held the gun in his hand.

"I am going to be open with you," he said. "I can't prove anything yet, but I am sure that this revolver was in the pocket of your housecoat when you went through the drawing room just after nine thirty. . . .

"I even wonder if at that particular moment you did not intend to kill your husband. . . . The testimony of the invalid on Rue du Cirque may help us to prove that. . . . You must have gone up to his door, didn't you? You heard voices, because your husband was talking to René Tortu at that time. . . .

"It then occurred to you to do a sort of substitution. . . . Would you not wound your husband just as deeply, if not more so, by killing Antoinette Vague instead of killing him? . . . Not counting the fact that, at the same time, you were casting suspicion on him.

"You have been preparing the ground since our talk yesterday. . . . You went on doing so today. . . .

"Under the pretext of looking for a stamp, or for writing paper, or something, you went into the secretary's office. She greeted you absently and went back to her work. . . .

"You saw the knife, which made the revolver unnecessary and was even better, since someone might hear the gun. . . ."

He stopped speaking, lit his pipe rather reluctantly, and stood there waiting. He had slipped the mother-of-pearl gun into his pocket. A long time went by. Madame Parendon's shoulders did not move. So she was not crying. She kept her back to him and, when she finally turned to look at him, her face was pale and frozen.

No one looking at her could have imagined what had taken place that morning on Avenue Marigny, and even less what had taken place in the overwhelming blue of the boudoir.

"I am not mad," she said emphatically.

He did not answer. What good would it have done? And besides, what did he know about it?

8

"Get yourself dressed, Madame," Maigret said gently. "You can pack a suitcase with a change of underwear and some personal belongings. . . . Perhaps you should ring for Lise?"

"To be sure that I won't commit suicide? Don't worry, there's no danger of that, but you may push the button on your right."

He waited for the maid to appear.

"Give Madame Parendon a hand. . . ."

Then he walked along the hallway, his head bowed, looking at the carpet. He lost his way, mistook one passage for another, and saw Ferdinand and fat Madame Vauquin through the glass door of the kitchen. There was an almost half-full bottle of red wine in front of Ferdinand. The butler had just poured himself a glass and was sitting with his elbows on the table, reading a newspaper.

He went in.

The other two were startled, and Ferdinand jumped to his feet at once.

"Would you give me a glass of wine, please?"

"I brought the other bottle from the office. . . ."

What did it matter? In the state he was in, vintage Saint-Emilion or some ordinary red wine . . .

He didn't dare say that he would have preferred the ordinary red.

He drank slowly, staring into space. He did not protest when the butler refilled his glass.

"Where are my men?"

"Waiting near the cloakroom. They didn't want to sit in the drawing room."

They were guarding the exit instinctively.

"Lucas, go back into the hallway where you were a few minutes ago. Stand outside the boudoir door and wait there for me."

He went back to see Ferdinand.

"Is the chauffeur in?"

"Do you want him? I'll call him right away."

"What I want is for him to be at the door with the car in a few minutes. . . . Are there any reporters waiting in the street?"

"Yes, sir."

"Photographers?"

"Yes."

He knocked at the door of Parendon's office. He was alone, sitting in front of scattered papers which he was annotating in red pencil. He saw Maigret and remained motionless, looking at him, not daring to ask any questions.

His blue eyes behind their thick lenses had an expression which combined softness and a sadness such as Maigret had rarely seen before.

Did he need to speak? The lawyer had understood. While waiting for the superintendent he had clung to his papers as if to a wreck.

"I think you will have one more occasion to study Article 64, Monsieur Parendon. . . ."

"Has she confessed?"

"Not yet."

"Do you think she will confess?"

"There will come a time, tonight, in ten days' time, or in a month, when she will crack; and I would rather not be present. . . ."

The little man took his handkerchief from his pocket and began to clean his glasses as if it were a matter of prime importance. Suddenly the irises of his eyes seemed to melt, to dissolve into the whites. Only his mouth remained, showing an almost childish emotion.

"Are you taking her away?"

His voice was scarcely audible.

"In order to avoid the reporters' comments and to give her departure some dignity, she will go by her own car. I shall give the instructions to the chauffeur, and we shall arrive at Police Headquarters at the same time."

Parendon gave him a look of gratitude.

"Do you want to see her?" asked Maigret, knowing what the answer would be.

"What could I say to her?"

"I know. You're right. Are the children here?"

"Gus is at school. I don't know if Bambi is in her room or if she has a class this afternoon. . . ."

Maigret was thinking both of the woman who was about to leave and of those who would be left behind. Life would be difficult for them too, for a time at least.

"Didn't she say anything about me?"

The lawyer asked the question timidly, almost fearfully.

"She spoke about you a great deal. . . ."

The superintendent understood now that Madame Parendon had not found the words which seemed to accuse her husband in books. They had been in herself. She had developed a kind of transference, projecting her own disturbance onto him.

He looked at his watch, and gave the reason for looking.

"I am giving her time to dress, to pack her suitcase. . . . The maid is with her. . . ."

". . . if the person charged with the commission of a felony or misdemeanor was then insane or acted by absolute necessity . . ."

Some men he had arrested because it was his job to do so had been acquitted by the court, others found guilty and sentenced. Some, especially at the beginning of his career, had been condemned to death, and two of them had asked him to be there at the final moment.

He had begun by studying medicine. He had regretted having to give it up because the circumstances so required. If he had been able to go on with it, would he not have chosen psychiatry?

In that case it would have been he who had to answer the question:

182

". . . if the person charged with the commission of a felony or misdemeanor was then insane or acted by absolute necessity . . ."

Perhaps he didn't regret the termination of his studies so much. He would not be required to decide.

Parendon got up and walked hesitantly, awkwardly, toward him and held out his little hand.

"I . . ."

But he was unable to speak. It was sufficient for them to shake hands silently, looking each other in the eye. Then Maigret went to the door, which he closed behind him without looking back.

He was surprised to see Lucas standing by the door with Torrence. A glance from his assistant in the direction of the drawing room explained why Lucas had left his post in the hall.

Madame Parendon stood there in the middle of the enormous room, dressed in a light-colored suit, with a hat and white gloves. Lise was standing behind her, holding a suitcase.

"You two go to the car and wait for me."

He felt that he was acting like a master of ceremonies, and he knew that he would always hate the moments he was living through.

He went toward Madame Parendon and bowed slightly. It was she who spoke, in a calm, natural voice.

"I shall follow you."

Lise went down with them in the elevator. The chauffeur rushed to open the car door and was surprised that Maigret did not follow his employer into the car.

He put the suitcase in the trunk.

"Drive Madame Parendon directly to 36, Quai des Orfèvres, go in through the archway, and turn left in the courtyard . . ."

"Very good, Superintendent."

Maigret gave the car time to break through the hedge of reporters, who had not understood what was happening. Then, while they bombarded him with questions, he rejoined Lucas and Torrence in the little black police car.

"Are you going to make an arrest, Superintendent?"

"I don't know. . . ."

"Do you know who's guilty?"

"I don't know. . . ."

He was being honest. The words of Article 64 came flooding into his memory one by one, terrifying in their imprecision.

The sun still shone, the chestnut trees were still growing greener, and he could see the same people prowling around the palace of the President of the Republic.